A View from the
BORDERLINE

A Collection of Short Stories

BY CHARLES SOUBY

ISBN   978-0-5785-9169-8
eISBN   978-0-5785-9173-5

Printed in the United States of America

Dedicated to:

Mark Langton, Tom Harper, Joe Fahy and Bob Ades.
Thanks for helping me stay sane during the
years I composed this anthology.

Acknowledgements:

A very special thanks to Mary Anne Maier for editing and proofreading this material; Lilliana Tannous, Benjamin Grant Bossi, Richard Olive, Lynne Celeste Gonzales and Paige Jenkins for walking with me as I developed these stories; Shastin Grace for the beautiful design and cover art; Oriana Murray, Amber Funk, Jim Souby and Betty Barton for taking time to review this manuscript and provide helpful feedback and James Tipton, as always, for helping me begin to grasp the craft of fiction and poetry.

Credits:

The Durschlag Twins first appeared in The Saturday Evening Post Online , November 14, 2014.

The Doberman Affair first appeared in eFiction Magazine, Volume 6, No. 3

The Plaid Golf Pants first appeared in eFiction Magazine, Volume 6, No. 10

Maypole Madness first appeared in The Opening Line, May 2013

CONTENTS

SILVER SLUM DOG

The power had been off for three days, and Leonard was damn frustrated. He tried to explain to the electric company gal on the phone that it was just a matter of a late paycheck, and he'd have the money in a week, but the woman brought up all the other late payments and then went into the whole "I'm so sorry you're having difficulties . . . blah, blah, blah."

The late check was actually an advance on Leonard's *next* paycheck because he blew his previous one at the racetrack bar. He met a redhead who threw off his timing. In fact, she was the one who finally brought him to ruin.

He was now certain she must have been a shill of the mobster guys who owned the place. He never actually met the owners but naturally assumed that anybody involved with such an enterprise had to be stinking villains of some sort. Still, he kept returning because he was smarter than they were. He had eyes and ears and a gut full of common sense.

Every time he got burned at the track, it was always the result of a woman barfly who would win over his attention at a crucial time in the betting. Instead of staying alert, Leonard would get lost in conversation, hoping against hope that he would finally get laid, have children, and live a happy life.

That redhead Hilda took the cake though. She was a tall, thirty-something siren who, upon entering the joint, looked straight at him as she slinked through the open glass doors of the bar overlooking the racetrack. There was a sense of command in her eyes that said she didn't want to fuck around. It was as if they were saying let's get down to business—you tell me who you are, I'll tell you who I am, and together we'll start a life—at least after some steamy sex at the Motel 6 over on Shreveport Avenue where all the bookies hang out.

She was bold in her entrance, and her gaze was so sultry he assumed she would sit down right beside him. Instead, she found a seat alone on the other side of the long, plush, horseshoe-shaped bar that glowed under a crystal chandelier. She stared straight ahead at nothing in front of her and ignored Leonard's ogle.

When the bartender approached her for a drink order, she finally glanced across the bar at Leonard, who called out, "Hey, Gussie, this one's on me, all right?"

The lady smiled contritely and looked at the bartender. Leonard couldn't hear what she had ordered, but it appeared as if Gus was fixing her a cosmopolitan. She raised her glass upon receipt of the drink, and Leonard followed suit. The whole exchange was arranged in a manner that would make it awkward and rude for him to immediately get up and walk over to the end of the bar to join her. Leonard had to wait for an invitation. The ball was now in her court, and he felt damn frustrated by the situation. In fact, this was exactly the kind of shit that always screwed him up at the track. Women and betting don't work well together. He had learned that long ago. And yet—here he was again.

He left the bar briefly to bet on the second race. Thorn Bird Legend was currently nine to one on the tote board, and Leonard had to get in on that action. When he returned, the redhead was on the stool next to his smoking a cigarette. He quickly changed his posture to that of a millionaire (or at least what he deemed to be a millionaire's posture—chest out, chin up, eyes straight ahead) and sat down next to her.

"Oh, thank God," she said. "I thought you had abandoned me."

Leonard descended into obnoxious snickering but tried to curtail it before he drove the woman out of the bar. This often happened with first contact. He'd either titter giddily or snicker through his nose. It would just happen—it was a mess.

The woman seemed taken aback but held her seat anyway.

"I'm sorry," Leonard said.

"Sorry for what?" asked the woman.

"I don't know."

Why was he sorry? Damn!

"I'm Leonard," he finally offered.

"I'm Hilda."

Leonard smiled, and Hilda smiled. There was a brief silence followed by Leonard's heavy breathing—he was trying to sigh, but it sounded perverse. Hilda still held to her seat.

"Do you come here often?" she asked.

"About twice a month," he said. "Whenever I feel inspired."

"What inspires you?"

"What? Oh, well, it's just a feeling I get when I look at the sports page. I know most all the horses, and there are some that I just feel an itch for on certain days." He took a sip of his drink. "When it's more than two horses and the odds are right at the start of the day, I go for it."

"Does your job allow for this adventurousness?"

"Yeah, I have a lot of latitude."

Leonard had a lot of latitude because he was off on a psych leave after a nervous breakdown he'd had at the AAA office where he worked in town. The perfumed fat lady who called herself his supervisor wouldn't let up on him one day, and he snapped. When they called him into the HR office, he claimed it was the chemicals in her cologne, and they had him evaluated by a psychiatrist who decided he needed six weeks off. He had already used up most of his sick time sneaking out to the track but had accrued a lot of extended emergency leave during his seventeen years as a AAA clerk. The HR people considered him a star employee and were happy to accommodate him. The reason they considered him a star employee was because they'd never heard of him. They naturally figured that anyone who could fly below the HR radar for seventeen years had to be a star. The only people at AAA who knew who he was were the perfumed fat lady and a couple of retired supervisors who were dead. The HR people loved Leonard so much that when he suggested that his psychiatric situation would cause him financial hardship, they quickly arranged for the payroll department to give him an advance on his pay.

"You must be quite a success," Hilda said, "if you can take days off from work to bet on the horses."

"Yeah, I'm considered pretty cool where I work. They look

to me for leadership. I'm a guy with intuition—a strong gut sense about things."

Hilda batted her eyelashes a couple of times. "Well what does your strong intuition tell you about me?"

Something inside Leonard wanted to say, "Trouble!" But it couldn't quite rise to the surface.

"I see a partner in crime," Leonard said. There was sing-songy lust in his voice. "I see someone who, like myself, gets pulled to the track because when that bell goes off at the gate, she knows it's signaling something far beyond fourteen horses running around a circle. It's signaling a new beginning—it's saying this time everything's gonna happen: love, success, and wild dreams come true." Leonard started snorting again and desperately tried to pull himself back, but his head was drooping down into his cocktail, and he must have looked mad as a hatter.

Hilda moaned in erotic ecstasy. She hummed like she had just discovered her winning exacta ticket. "Oh you, you," she said. "You're the one!"

Just then, the sound of the bells went off. He abruptly turned to the TV to watch Thorn Bird Legend, whose line had remained steady on the board all the way to the post. It was a close race, Thorn Bird was lagging in third place for most of it, and Leonard had bet him to win. Sure enough, though, during the home stretch he shot ahead by a nose, and Leonard announced that he had a thousand bucks waiting for him at the window.

Now he was snorting like a wild boar. It was uncontrollable. The only thing that kept him from completely repulsing his red-haired ticket to paradise was that she was screaming too. She grabbed him and kissed him profusely on the cheek and he could feel her lipstick peel off and smear onto the side of his face.

Leonard grabbed his drink and gulped it up. He reached for hers and shoved it in her face until she took it and poured it down the hatch.

"Two more, Gussie, and make 'em strong!"

Hilda was yelping, "Woo hoo, woo hoo!"

A minute later, Gus set two drinks in front of them. Leonard forked over a twenty-dollar bill and grabbed the drinks, handing the cosmopolitan to Hilda.

"Here's to how," he said. They both tilted their drinks up and drained them in one gulp. Gus was standing in front of the couple and immediately grabbed the empty glasses unsolicited and took them back to the well to fill up once more.

"So what do we do now?" Hilda asked.

"We wait, is what we do. The seventh race is the key. Angry Turk is sixteen to one but I guarantee he'll at least place. But it's the *eighth* race I'm waiting on—Silver Slum Dog, twenty-five to one. I'm betting on him with all my loot. I'm betting him to win. I just know it. It's his day."

"That's so exciting that you know that!" she said.

"Oh, I know it all right. The seventh and eight races are my meal ticket, baby; Thorn Bird was just an hors d'oeuvre." Leonard chortled as Hilda smiled.

"All this fast drinking is getting me goosepimply," Hilda said.

"Just the excitement of the track, darling. I don't let it

control me though. That's the key. We just had our little cele-bration, and now we need to buckle down and focus until the seventh race."

"Focus on what?"

Leonard looked off at the sky dreamily for a second and then smiled and turned to Hilda. "Focus on each other," he said.

Hilda picked up her drink and coerced Leonard to click glasses with her. They both took big gulps, and suddenly Leon-ard was drunk.

"Oh shit," he said.

"What, what did I do?" Hilda feigned deep hurt.

"Nothing, babe. It's just I try not to let myself get out of control with the booze; it affects my betting."

"Why should it?"

"I don't know. It just does." Leonard tried to reacquire his equilibrium. He decided to focus on his babe. "So what are you doing here, Hilda?"

Hilda sighed like a schoolgirl who's been asked to share her life story. She was still gorgeous to Leonard, but now a glow of humanness slipped through the cracks of her beguiling charm.

"I work for Lloyd's of London as a secretary, and every cou-ple of months I take a workday off to bet on a horse for my boss. It's a tradition. He sends me out here with five hundred dollars and says to go to it. I always pick a winner. It's in my blood—just like my mother. She was a bingo champion."

"We have so much in common."

"Yes, that's how I felt from the moment I saw you."

"So tell me. What horse are you betting on, anyway?"

"Oh, it doesn't work that way. I don't study the sheets or anything. Somewhere around the fifth race I just glance up at the board and pick a name I like a lot. Sometimes I pick a favorite and sometimes I pick a long shot."

Leonard started shaking his head. "Well, that's no way to do it."

"What do you mean? It usually works; I win. I'll show you on the fifth race." Hilda reached her hand over and started mussing up Leonard's hair, and then they both sipped their drinks and stared at each other seductively. Leonard hated small talk, but he knew it was the price to pay for companionship. He asked her about Lloyd's of London, and she asked him about his job. AAA was such an impressive American institution to be part of, she said, and he must be very proud. Lloyd's of London was OK too except that it was British—hence the name. There wasn't nearly the same pride there. She said she sometimes felt like Benedict Arnold.

When the fifth race came up, Hilda looked up at the board in the bar and immediately announced, "Snowball Slushy. That's the one."

Leonard shook his head. He'd seen Snowball Slushy in the paper for over a year; she never did anything. Snowball Slushy was what he thought of as a "filler" horse. They trotted her out to the gate so the others had an extra body to run against. She was always something like fifteen to one even though her odds weren't even that good. That afternoon, in fact, she *was* fifteen to one as the names came up on the board.

"I'm sorry, Leonard. I have to do this." She pushed herself off the bar and, staggering slightly, made her way out and down to the betting windows.

Leonard was now unpleasantly drunk and didn't know how he was going to make it to the seventh race let alone the eight, where his next two picks were waiting.

Hilda was gone an especially long time but returned just as the horses stepped up to the starting gate. She sat down next to Leonard with her back facing the bar so she could see the big TV, which hung on the wall above the huge windows looking out onto the track.

"Kiss me for good luck, Leonard."

Leonard let his face fall into hers and they were suddenly into a sloppy, lusty kiss until the starting bell pulled them apart.

To Leonard's great surprise, Snowball Slushy was tightly in with the frontrunners through the first turn and beyond. He was holding third place consistently but nosed into second a couple of times.

"You bet on him to show, right?" Leonard asked.

"No. To win, baby, to win!" She bounced up and down humping the barstool like she was Snowball's jockey. "Go, Ballsy, go! Go, Ballsy! Go, Ballsy!"

As they headed into the final stretch, Snowball Slushy suddenly pushed ahead. Hilda screamed out in ear-shattering shrillness as her horse crossed the finish line almost a full length ahead of her competition.

She turned to Leonard, and they kissed wildly and openly in front of the small but growing bar crowd. Their tongues were like two frogs warring over a single fly. Finally, she slid off the stool and out of the bar to pick up her fortune.

Leonard slumped on the bar. He looked around, and everybody was staring at him. He looked back at his drink and grabbed it, taking a good strong pull. He looked at his watch, but his mind was going foggy. He couldn't remember how long it was until the seventh race.

Hilda barreled back into the bar ten minutes later clutching her purse. "We're rich, lover!" she screamed.

"I'm drunk," Leonard said.

"Get over it. You've got horses to bet on. I'm not supporting you; you need to stand on your own two feet."

"It's Angry Turk in the seventh," Leonard blurted out.

"Yes! I love it! Angry Turk!" Hilda began rubbing Leonard's shoulders and then looked over at the bartender, who was mixing drinks. "Gussie," she said. "Get us another pair, would you, love?"

Gus looked at Hilda and nodded his head. A moment later, after fixing some drinks for a slinky, blonde waitress, he grabbed glasses from out of the well and filled them with ice.

When Leonard looked up, Gus had set two drinks in front of each of them.

"What's this?" Leonard asked.

Gus looked at him with umbrage. "She said, 'Get us another pair,' so I did."

"No," Hilda giggled. "I meant a pair as in one for each of us. But that's all right. I'm rich!" She was wobbling on her barstool but stuffed her hand in her purse and pulled out two twenty dollar bills.

Leonard looked at her. "I thought it was your boss's money."

"It is, but we split it fifty-fifty."

Gus took the money and walked over to the cash register.

Leonard pulled himself back up and took a swig off of his drink.

"Now what do we do?" Leonard asked.

"We wait is what we do," Hilda said.

"Oh, that's right. We wait."

And so they waited. The two of them took their drinks from the bar and cozied up next to each other at a curved vinyl booth against the wall where they could look out the window and watch the horses run around the track. Hilda pulled out a racing form and started studying the seventh race.

"I like Roosevelt's Nephew."

"Franklin's or Teddy's?"

"No, no, the *horse*, silly. I like Roosevelt's Nephew in the seventh."

"That's ridiculous. Who is he, anyway?" Leonard let his head drop down and rub against Hilda's bosom so he could look at the racing form close up. "No," he said. He lifted his head back up. "That's ridiculous. It's Angry Turk in the seventh."

"You said Angry Turk to place. I say Roosevelt's Nephew to win."

"It's your money."

"I'm on a roll, and you're drunk."

Leonard leaned back against the back of the vinyl sofa. Hilda leaned back and kissed his cheek several times, and then they started making out, fondling each other under the table. In no time it was the seventh race, and the two of them pulled themselves away from each other and out of the booth. They left the bar and stumbled down to the betting windows.

"So I'm going to show you how to do this," Leonard said as they staggered down the stairs. "It's Angry Turk to win."

"Do as you please; it's your money. I say Roosevelt's Nephew to win and Angry Turk to place. Who's favored anyway?"

"Molly Tenbrooks."

"OK, then. I bet Roosevelt's Nephew to win, Angry Turk to place and Molly Tenbrooks to show. That's my trifecta, baby!"

Leonard shook his head and laughed at Hilda.

"Why are you being so mean to me?" Hilda asked. "I feel like I don't know you anymore." She stormed away from Leonard to a window at the other end of the long row.

Leonard started to follow her, but a window opened in front of him and he fell into it. After collecting on Thorn Bird Legend, he placed his bet—Angry Turk to win. He bet everything he had and then pulled out his checkbook and emptied his bank account. He muttered strange words to the cashier but couldn't quite remember what it was he wanted to say—something about Hilda.

As he turned from the window, Hilda walked right past him. She had her nose up, and after a moment of contemplation, Leonard followed her upstairs to the bar. Hilda took her original seat at the far end of the bar and ordered a cosmopolitan. Leonard sat at his original seat but stared across the bar at her with pouty lips like he was remorseful. Hilda caught him in a quick glance and sighed. She grabbed her drink and walked back over to his side and sat down next to him.

"I'm sorry for what I said," Leonard said. "I was just trying to make a point. That's how my dad always did it with me. He'd tell me I was stupid to make sure he got my attention."

"Oh, you poor thing." Hilda kissed him on top of his head. Leonard thought he could feel the rest of her lipstick peeling off onto his hair.

Suddenly the bell went off and they both turned to the TV behind them and watched the race.

"Roosevelt, Turk, and Tenbrooks," Molly screamed as they made the first turn. "Roosevelt, Turk and Tenbrooks!"

"Angry Turk, baby. Angry Turk!" Leonard shouted.

The horses ripped around the track to the final turn. Angry Turk held the lead down the final stretch with Roosevelt and Molly in close tow. Leonard felt guilty that he hadn't been a little more forceful with Hilda, but she had to learn. We all have to learn the hard way sooner or later.

Angry Turk was flying down the home stretch like the champion of champions when in a stunning turn of events, Roosevelt's Nephew seemed to become possessed with a cosmic flash of energy and charged up upon the leader.

"No!" Leonard screamed.

"Yes!" Hilda screamed.

Roosevelt's Nephew was now being jockeyed from on high and suddenly shot ahead, beating Angry Turk at the finish line by a nose, followed by Molly Tenbrooks.

Hilda let loose a bloodcurdling scream that almost brought the chandelier down.

"Son of a bitch!" Leonard yelled.

"I'm rich!" Hilda screamed. "I bet everything at fifteen to one. Oh happy day at Lloyd's of London!"

"I'm ruined!" screamed Leonard.

"Oh, love, I'm so sorry, but you'll get it back on the eight race. You said you would."

"I'm broke." Leonard's head fell down onto the bar.

"Gussie, get my friend a drink. I think he's failing." She turned to Leonard. "It's all right, love. A little drinky-winky will take care of everything. It always does!"

Gus put a drink in front of Leonard, and he hoisted it up and down his throat. Hilda watched with great sympathy.

"Gussy, another for Leonard, please. Make it a double." Gus was back in front of them quickly as Hilda reached into her purse and pulled out another twenty from her wallet.

"Hilda, you got to lend me a few bucks—just enough to get my money back. Hell, a hundred is all I need."

"Oh, Lenny darling, I can't do that. It would haunt you for the rest of your life. Besides, I could never be with a man who can't support himself."

"Oh, please, Hilda. Anything. Fifty dollars. Please."

Hilda frowned and huffed. "I'm heartbroken, Lenny. I never thought it would come to this. I thought you were a strong man—self-confident, a leader, an *American*."

"Oh, but I am. I've just fallen on some bad luck in the seventh."

"I'm sorry, Leonard. I'm not a welfare agency. It's over between us." She picked up her freshly poured drink, lifted it to her mouth, drained it, and walked out of the bar.

Leonard was undone again. He seemed to fade away into a blackout and when he came to, he reached for his drink as he heard the bells ring for the eight race. His ears followed the horses all the way around the track until the announcer said, "It's Silver Slum Dog by a nose. What an upset!"

GODOT MEETS GUFFMAN

It was Cindy's first time at the front desk. Mrs. Falstaff had quit the day before, and Cindy was reassigned to be temporary lunchtime receptionist while they searched for a new employee. Mrs. Albertson—usually the backup—was now handling reception duties for the bulk of the day, but she was also personal assistant to Jeremy Farber, the co-founder and chief investigator. Jeremy had determined that at seventeen, Cindy was too young to exhibit the grace and poise of a front desk receptionist for a PI firm. Instead, she was assigned busywork in the back office.

Cindy thought Mrs. Falstaff was a bit of a baby for running off, but the truth was, nobody really wanted the job. A private investigation business was not a place where you typically meet happy people coming in to celebrate life. The work was stressful and depressing, and since Mrs. Falstaff was married into wealth and not especially desperate for income, she just up and quit one day when things got edgy. Cindy despised people like her.

Cindy had taken the job as office intern prior to her senior year at San Gabriel High School. She was fascinated by the private investigation field and had discerned through her strong social studies skills—she had gotten A's in both of Mr. Kipling's classes—that information management and intelligence were to become the most prolific and profitable job markets of the future. Her parents felt her potential career path would end up in disaster—that she should get an MBA instead—but they agreed to let her take the job to get her out of the house for the summer as well as possibly lead her to see the error of her ambitions.

Typically, Cindy's job was to collect and collate data for Jeremy and his partner, Goose Gossage—"not to be confused with the Hall of Fame baseball player," he always explained. It turned out neither of the PIs was like Thomas Magnum from Cindy's favorite TV reruns. They were more like tender-footed tennis stars. Both men had served their country in the first Gulf War. They met while doing work for Army Intel and fell in love with the field. They also fell in love with each other. Goose and Jeremy were a gay couple who, during the early years of their careers, had been active in repealing "Don't Ask, Don't Tell." Initially, their activism hurt business because they were dependent upon referrals from fellow vets and military contacts, and most of them Didn't Really Want to Know.

Cindy didn't really want to know either, but not for any reason other than that she had her own love issues. She was relieved to be working for a gay couple, though, because she typically had discomfort around older men. It was not because older men hit on her (although one of her teachers, Dr. Cornwall, did in the hallway outside study hall), but it seemed most straight older men treated her like their adolescent daughter. They didn't acknowledge her blossoming adult sensibilities the way she would have liked. One of her neighbors once told her she had a "youthful Parker Posey quality" that made her fun to look at and listen to. Cindy didn't know what that meant but assumed it was a bad thing because the neighbor always asked her stupid kid questions.

Cindy read about self esteem in a psychology magazine she found at the orthodontist's office and figured out that if people treat you like a kid, you stay a kid. And if you stay a kid, no boys, particularly athletes like Jonathan Portman, captain of the soccer team, will want to marry you. This was a serious concern for her since, at seventeen, she was fast approaching that age where if she didn't land a husband soon, she might be out of luck for the rest of her life.

One of her fantasies was that Jonathan Portman would marry another girl—Missy Thompson, for example, who was always chasing after him—but then would become suspicious of her and hire Cindy as his private investigator. Within a few days, Cindy would catch Missy making out with some sleazy drug addict in his dope palace hotel room in Hayward, and she'd bring photos back to Jonathan. They'd make love, and she'd blackmail Missy into a mess-free divorce so she and Jonathan could move to the Bahamas, where she would be the Magnum PI of the Caribbean. She'd often take her three children along with her when investigating major cases, as they'd serve as a perfect cover.

Cindy spent a good ten minutes in the bathroom prior to coming out to the front desk, which annoyed Mrs. Albertson, who was in a hurry to get to lunch.

"When you are asked to be somewhere at a specific time, you jolly well better be there," she said.

"Yes, Mrs. Albertson. I just want to look my best."

Mrs. Albertson ignored the comment. She was probably jealous that no amount of time in the bathroom could make her look as young and appealing as Cindy.

"The office will be empty, dear. If you get a phone call or a visitor, all you need to do is take down a name and a phone number and tell them we'll get back to them soon."

Mrs. Albertson walked back to her cubicle and returned with her coat and purse. Jeremy and Goose followed behind her.

"Remember what I told you about smiling when you're talking on the phone," Goose said with a big grin. "It projects to the clients and makes them happy they called."

"Yes, sir, Goose. I've started doing that at home, and it really works." Cindy was beaming like an eight-year-old who got an "A" on her spelling test. It occurred to her as she was smiling that she herself might be responsible for old people treating her like an adolescent.

Goose smiled back. "You're a blossoming young lady, Cindy," he said and then walked out the door into the hallway of the early twentieth-century office building. Cindy loved those halls. They seemed permeated with the aura of Sam Spade, Miles Archer, and that 1930s LA guy.

Cindy spent the first couple of minutes at the front desk positioning herself. She learned in computer class all the ergonomic tricks of desk presence. She carefully reached out to make sure the phone was less than an arms-length away. There was no wrist protector for either her keyboard or mouse pad, but that was OK because she was not required to do research on the computer anyway. Or was she? What if they expected the Hatteberg account to be set up while they were gone? She was about to go and grab the new folder from the back when she realized she should not leave the front desk under any circumstances.

"Oh, crap," she said, just as a reflection appeared through the frosted glass of the front door. A UPS man walked in carrying a box and an electronic tracker. He carried the box behind the counter and laid it down next to Cindy's desk. He held out his electronic device and a little plastic marking stick.

"Sign here, please."

"I don't know if I'm allowed to."

"Of course you are," the man said. "I don't give a shit who signs."

The office door opened again, and a nervous-looking man in his mid-forties stepped in. He was dark and handsome, with a thin black mustache, and was wearing a clean-and-pressed gray raincoat. He had a plaid scarf around his neck and was also wearing a fedora. She glanced at him and then back at the deliveryman.

"Sir, I was told to get names and phone numbers, not sign for packages. What if there are subpoenas in the box?"

"Lady, I've been coming here for nine years. Nobody has ever refused to sign for a package. A twelve-year-old boy once signed for a package. Please sign the goddamn thing."

Cindy grabbed the tracker and the little stick pen thing and scribbled her name on the screen.

"Thank you," said the deliveryman as he turned to walk out. She couldn't see it but knew he had rolled his eyes at the stranger who was now approaching the counter in front of her.

She gathered herself and took a deep breath.

"Hi," she said.

Cindy was trying to hold back the excitement of meeting her first client at the front desk.

"How do you do," the man said. There was a touch of soft worry in his voice.

"Everybody's gone for lunch," she said. "I mean . . . what can I do for you?"

"I'm trying to track down Jeremy Farber."

Cindy started giggling. "That's ironic."

"What's ironic?"

"You're trying to track down a private investigator."

The man laughed nervously but became serious again.

"I assume this is his office?"

"Yeah, I mean yes." She pointed to the front door where the reflection of "Farber and Gossage" shown backward through the frosted glass.

"You say everybody's at lunch?"

"Yes, but I'll take your number, and he can call you back soon."

"I don't have my cell phone, but I could come back tomor-row. I'd like to speak with him sooner though."

"Do you have a contract with us?"

"No, but I'll sign one right now. I was referred to Jeremy by a guy I served with in the Gulf War."

"Yes. Jeremy was in the Gulf War."

The man sneered momentarily like he was being mocked and then stared at her blankly. She seemed to be just now coming into focus.

"How old are you?"

"Seventeen years old as of last February."

He shook his head.

"You're a bit obtuse, aren't you?"

"Yeah, I guess." She stared blankly into his eyes.

He sighed. "That's all right. Young men find that kind of thing attractive. I know I did when I was seventeen. I thought it was almost mystical."

"Oh, cool."

The man sighed again as he stood across the wood-stained counter from Cindy. He seemed to be pondering how to best approach the present situation.

"Listen," he said. "A couple of days ago, my friend phoned Jeremy, who said he'd be glad to take my case; it's just that I've got a bunch of stuff to do over the next two days, and then I'm flying back to Chicago. Can you do, like, an intake interview with me or whatever it is you people do?"

"OK, but you have to promise not to tell anybody."

Cindy realized the absurdity of what she had just said and blushed and giggled. She opened a couple of desk drawers and looked inside. After rummaging, she found a box of Pentel pens and a stack of spiral notebooks. She waved a notebook at the man, who turned and walked over to one of two leather chairs that sat next to a coffee table to the right of the front door.

Cindy grabbed her notebook and a pen and walked around the counter and joined the man at the chairs. Before they sat down, the man held out his hand, and Cindy shook it.

"My name is Sal Barber," he said. "I grew up around here— in Menlo Park. I graduated from Portola Valley Country Day

School and—"

"Oh. That's a private school! You must be rich."

"Yes, we were comfortable growing up." He looked at Cindy with some doubt. "Listen, maybe I would be better off waiting for Jeremy to come back. This is involved and might seem a little . . . silly to you. You're young and full of possibilities. When you get to my age, doors start slamming shut."

"Oh, no. You can't let them slam shut! Then there's no hope for anybody."

"Excuse me?"

"Kids look up to you grownups for guidance. I mean, I'm not a kid. I'm a grownup myself, but I depend on you to give me a sense that life will fulfill me one day."

"Yes, that's all well and good, but when you lose somebody whom you loved with your heart and soul, there's not a lot of point being a role model anymore."

"Your wife died?"

"No, I'm not married, and nobody died. You see, that's why I'm here. But I'm thinking I should just wait and meet with Jeremy to discuss this."

"If it's about love, I think I can probably relate more than Jeremy unless you're gay. He and Goose are gay."

"Can we step outside so I can have a cigarette?"

Cindy was silent as she weighed the pros and cons of leaving the office unattended. There were no real pros at all except that she would be helping a man tell his story, and the customer is always right, or so her father taught her. The cons were that she would be fired, but nobody was due back for an hour, so unless there were extenuating circumstances, she could always cover her tracks, and this seemed to be an emergency.

The two of them got up from their chairs and walked out of the office to the elevator and down to the main front entrance, where there were ornate, brass fixtures on the walls and two metal-framed glass doors that led out into the warm, bright noonday sun. Cars rushed by, and a kid on a bicycle rode past them on the sidewalk as they found their way to the bench along the curb of the street.

"I hate people riding bicycles on sidewalks," Cindy said. "It's so rude."

The two of them sat down as Sal reached inside his raincoat for his cigarettes, a pack of Camel filters. He pulled one out and then stuck the pack back into his coat and pulled out a metal flip-top lighter.

"It's a little warm for a raincoat, isn't it?" Cindy asked.

"It was foggy earlier, and this was the only thing I brought on my trip that was warm."

"It's very nice."

"So, here's the story. I had a girlfriend in high school, and we were on the verge of getting married. It was the happiest time of my life."

Cindy smiled involuntarily, like she understood.

"Do you have a boyfriend?"

"No. I like a guy though."

"You should seize the day, my dear." He took a drag of his cigarette. "The teen years are a crazy time, a time of uncertainty, but they can also be the happiest time of your life."

"If they're the happiest time of my life, what do I have to live for?"

"You're a very precocious young lady."

"Is that good?"

"Yes. Anyway, her name was Alicia, and she resembled you in many ways—dark hair and an innocent, youthful face full of curiosity. She was much like that movie actress Parker Posey—in her younger years—a little stupid, but in a sweet sort of way, you know, like in that *Guffman* movie. Not that you're stupid."

"I'm obtuse."

"That was a wrong choice of words." Sal took another pull from his cigarette. "Anyway, we graduated in 1990, and together we decided to take a year off to find ourselves. Our parents hated that. Mine had expectations I would go to law school, and Alicia's parents wanted her to get an MBA."

"That's a business degree."

"Yes, thank you. The two of us scraped our pennies together and got a pair of plane tickets to Paris. We rented a studio apartment on Rue de Louvois, and I found a job stocking shelves at Galeries Lafayette, an upscale French department store. She was hired at a seafood market deboning fish. It was difficult for both of us because we didn't speak French very well. We weren't allowed to interact with the public."

"Me neither."

"Then in August, Saddam Hussein invaded Kuwait—"

"He was a bad man."

"Yes, very bad—"

"He attacked New York and flew airplanes into—"

"No, no, that wasn't him."

"Are you sure?"

"Yes. Anyway, when he invaded Kuwait, I was outraged;

I felt personally attacked, and it was all the more frustrating because the French, though not delighted by the situation, seemed to react like 'c'est la vie.'"

"Such is life!"

"Exactly! I wanted to teach that son of a bitch a lesson he'd never forget. I hoped and prayed to God that President Bush—the older one—would start a war, and we could wipe him off the face of the earth."

"We did! I saw it on TV. We hung him."

"Yes, it was a truly satisfying day for me, I must say."

"I remember when he was walking out to the wooden platform—"

"To the gallows."

"Yeah, the gallows. Some angry man yelled nasty things at him, and he yelled nasty things back. I remember thinking that if he could just have held his temper, he might not be in a situation like that in the first place. You know what I mean?"

"People like him are born to lose their tempers, and then they make us all lose our tempers. It's the way of the world."

"C'est la vie."

"Yes."

"Ironic. So what happened to Alicia?"

"That's what I'm getting to. As soon as we declared war— well we didn't actually *declare* war—but as soon as Operation Desert Shield was announced, I decided I would go back home and enlist. Alicia was beside herself. We came to France to get away from that madness, she said. I told her you can't run from a thing like that. You can't just wave it off like a Frenchman. It will follow you everywhere, like your own soul."

"Wow, that's heavy."

"Yes, truth has a heavy weight to it."

"May I try a cigarette?"

Sal reached inside his coat and pulled out his pack and tapped a cigarette out for Cindy. She put it to her mouth, and he lit it. She took a couple of light puffs but didn't inhale the smoke into her lungs.

"The day I left Paris was the hardest day of my life. Alicia cried and cried as she watched me pack my suitcases, and she refused to come with me to the airport. She called me all sorts of unspeakable names and wouldn't hug me when I left. I felt absolutely miserable and realized that serving your country is the hardest thing a man can do."

"That sounds terrible. She was so insensitive—but if you had died she would have been left alone."

"It was as if *she* had died." Sal let his cigarette drop out of his hand onto the ground and then put it out with his right heel and kicked it into the curb. Cindy stared down at his black, shiny shoes.

"I sent her letters from Fort Benning, but she never answered them. I was heartbroken and decided that it was my destiny to be a suicide machine for the US Army. If any of my comrades were to fall into trouble, I would throw myself into the enemy and blow them up with hand grenades."

"Oh, that's so romantic!"

"I fantasized that Alicia was being held by Arabs and that I'd track them down in Baghdad. I'd scale the walls of a building and sneak into the room where she was being held captive. She'd be tied up in ropes, and I'd cut her free. Just as she was escaping, the enemy would find us. Just like with my comrades, I would run into them with a grenade and give my life for my true love."

"You can only do that once, you know."

"Yes, but it turned out the war wasn't like that. The Iraqis were a bunch of wussies; they ran from us with their hands in the air. I hated them for their lack of commitment."

"They sound like Mrs. Falstaff."

"Six months in," Sal continued, "I was allowed to take my first leave, and I flew to Paris to find Alicia. She had moved out of the apartment on Rue de Louvois and left no forwarding address. I telephoned her parents long distance to see if she had gone back home, but they hadn't heard from her in months. All they knew was that I broke her heart. Her father supported my decision to fight for my country in the Middle East, but her mother thought I was heartless and told me to never call there again. I tried hard to explain how badly I had suffered without her, but it was to no avail."

"So did you go back to Iraq?"

"To Kuwait, yes. I served there and then back in the States for two years. Kuwait was a barren and desperate place. If it weren't for the oil wells, nobody would have wanted it. Sometimes, I admit, I cursed my government for sending us on a wild-goose chase to protect petroleum interests, but then I would snap back and remember that we're all in this together."

"Arabs too?"

"I guess."

Cindy put her cigarette out in the same manner that Sal had, and then he reached into his coat and pulled out another one for himself and lit it.

"You smoke a lot, Mr. Barber."

"Call me Sal. And yes, it's one of the sad by-products of warfare."

"After my two years were up, I flew back to the States and came home to Menlo Park to live with my family. Alicia's parents wouldn't answer my calls and even threatened to get a restraining order against me if I came by their house. I spoke to several of our mutual friends from high school, and even though no one admitted to hearing from her, they said that they were pretty certain she had remained in Europe and was studying international law.

"Over the next several months, I spent a fortune on long-distance phone calls—this was before there were cell phones—calling schools throughout Europe to see if she was enrolled, but nobody had heard of her, or they didn't speak English very well. It was frustrating. I would have broken into her parents' home to see if I could find letters she had written, but my sense of honor as a veteran kept me from doing something that drastic."

Cindy thought about how nobody sent letters anymore. It was very sad.

"So, finally, three months ago I ran into Mike Mahoney, who was living in Chicago. He was my very best friend in high school, but we had lost touch after I went to Paris with Alicia. We had drinks together on Rush Street one evening, and he told me that he had heard Alicia was somewhere back here in California advocating for American veterans. I was stunned. Of all the things she could be doing with her life."

"Maybe she was doing this in your memory."

"I thought about that when Mike told me, and while he was in the bathroom, I tried to contact her parents on my cell phone, but their number had been disconnected. When Mike came back to the table, I told him what I had just done, and he said her folks had long since retired and moved to Orange County somewhere."

"I'm moving to the Bahamas one day, but I won't have to retire because I'll already be there."

Sal stopped speaking and stared at Cindy in silence. For a moment she stared back but then looked down, drenched in an undefined guilt. She felt herself fall into a deep and troubled chasm in her soul that told her she was not enough and never could be.

"You know," Sal said, "as I sit here, I realize you are so much like Alicia. She spoke the same way as you, made the same observations. It's almost uncanny."

Cindy's eyes watered. She felt disconnected with the world.

"It's probably because we're both like Parker Posey," she said. "Do you suppose that's a good thing?"

"I don't know."

"Is Parker Posey obtuse?"

"I've never met her. I only know her from her old 1990s movie characters."

"Could you imagine living with her?"

"I'm not certain."

"If you were a varsity soccer player, could you imagine marrying Parker Posey?"

"If I were in high school I suppose I could, but I don't

know anymore."

"Really? If you were in high school?"

Sal smiled. Cindy's tears seemed to awaken a new tenderness in him.

"Sure I would. If I was in high school, I'd marry Parker Posey in a hot second."

Cindy smiled and took a deep breath.

"Well, shoot," Cindy said, "I don't really know how to proceed with this interview thing. I've never done an intake before."

"You've done a magnificent job, Cindy. You really have. I'll tell you what; I'm going back to my hotel to make a couple of calls. Maybe I'll see you later—or maybe not. You should probably get back up to the office. You never know what kind of cases are waiting for you."

Cindy held out her hand shyly, and Sal shook it. She stood up from the bench, smiled at him again, and walked away. She was filled with an odd, melancholy happiness as she strolled back to the office building. She wondered if her best years lay ahead or if they were where she was right now.

THE PARABLE OF THE NERD & THE ANTELOPE

Young Bundy McPherson was a savant. His family and neighbors thought there was something frightfully troubling about him, and thus, like so many youth, he was sadly misunderstood.

To be clear, though, this is not Bundy's story. He merely set in motion a series of events that will be described herein. Once his part is completed, he will be absented from the narrative.

The deal with Bundy was that he was an animal whisperer—horses, dogs, cats, and wildlife. This divine gift was a sight to behold. For example, he would wander into his family's backyard in Downers Grove, Illinois, and strike up remarkable conversations with raccoons that hung around the garbage cans in the evening. After a cordial chat, the raccoons would disperse, and he would continue his wanderings.

During the daytime, squirrels, birds, and stray cats would approach him in small groups underneath an oak tree, and he would update them on the recent goings-on. They wouldn't bother to update him, but only because nothing was ever going on—it was always the same routine. The animals were content in their simple world, and Bundy lived vicariously through their contentment.

Bundy also had a very profound sense of justice. He was regularly bullied in grade school due to his dorky, freckled face and horn-rimmed glasses. After years of abuse, his heart demanded retribution. One could imagine a Hollywood movie where Bundy the Savant puts together an angry posse of wild animals who show up at school during recess and slaughter all the tough boys that made his and his fellow dorks' lives miserable—something like Jack Hanna meets *Carrie*. But to his credit, Bundy had a deep fraternal love for his critter friends, so he would certainly never expose them to rocks and sticks and, ultimately, policemen's guns.

This story begins when the McPhersons took a family safari to Tanzania during the summer before Bundy started seventh grade.

In Africa, Bundy had the opportunity to make a wide variety of new animal friends, most of which he had never seen outside the Brookfield Zoo in Chicago.

The safari guide took the McPhersons on several jeep rides across the Serengeti Plain, where Bundy watched the most amazing display of free-range joyousness he could ever imagine.

One species that intrigued him was the African antelope. He had never seen such a graceful and truly harmonious collective of animals in his life. He longed to commune with them privately, but alas, the tour guide kept him restrained with grave references to the dangers of the African savanna.

So it was that on their fourth day of touring, Bundy saw what was surely the most horrific sight of his life. A large herd of antelope was grazing by a nest of trees. The little ones were playing and minding their own business when, out of nowhere, a pack of lions jumped them and began tearing one of the fawns to shreds. This scene was all the more horrifying due to the fact that the McPherson's' tour guide relished in the slaughter and explained to the family what a rare treat it was to see such a brilliant act of nature take place firsthand from less than fifty yards away.

"Praise Allah," the tour guide said. "We have been blessed to behold a true wonder of nature."

Bundy felt neither blessed, nor beholden, nor amused by the situation. It was a moment of pure brutality—an injustice in nature of the highest order—and he swore right then and there he would bring this ugly charade to an end.

Here, the reader needs to be reminded that this story is not about Bundy; he is merely the instigator of the story's upcoming events. This fact is repeated again only because it would be a great disappointment to expect an entire African adventure involving a twelve-year-old savant and then discover that the boy had removed himself to the Chicago suburbs while the reader is stuck in backwoods Tanzania.

For the rest of the afternoon following the "massacre on the savanna," as Bundy called it, he spent his time brooding and plotting. Finally, he came up with a plan that would put his God-given skills to good purpose.

Late in the evening he snuck out of his tent, and after rustling around through campground paraphernalia, he found a set of keys and stole the safari guide's jeep.

Within a half hour of traversing the dark dusty roads of the plains, he found himself at the exact location where the sickening events of that day had occurred. He parked the vehicle a ways off the road on the dark grassy plains and wandered on foot as a full moon lit the savanna. He shortly found the familiar island of trees and started calling for the antelope to make themselves present. He was unsure whether he would be inviting danger to them, as he had been unable to discern whether lions were nocturnal animals, but in a sense that was the whole point.

Because of Bundy's great talent, he was shortly attended by a group of antelope, three families in fact, that joined him in friendly conversation. Bundy was stunned to find out that the antelope had completely forgotten the day's events, and even the fawn's mother was now only vaguely mourning the loss of her adorable little daughter.

"You've got to do something," Bundy said. "This madness has to stop."

The antelope were bewildered by Bundy's rant because never in anyone's life had such a concept been planted in their minds. In truth, no concepts had ever been planted in their minds. They typically hung out feeding and playing except when danger was near; then they ran for dear life until the coast was clear.

Bundy was a patient boy and stood firm among the antelope, proposing strategy as best he could. The antelope must engineer a way to bait and trap the lions, he explained. They must punish them for the evil deeds they had done—render them lame, maybe even execute some of them. Soon all lions would learn never to bother the antelope again.

At first recital, the plan was rather flimsy, and the reader need not be subjected to its stupidity, but Bundy knew that with some tweaking and evolution, these soft and gentle prey would master their destiny and be liberated.

Confident that he had done the right thing, Bundy retreated back to camp, where he was severely reprimanded by his family for stealing the jeep. This was, of course, after his mother finished sobbing, for she was certain he had been eaten by a herd of rhinos or hippos or—God forbid—lions.

In fear for Bundy's safety and mental health, the McPhersons immediately packed up and left for Kenya. They flew out of Nairobi the following day, never to return to the great continent of Africa.

The rest of Bundy's life was rather unremarkable. He managed to marry a sweet, blonde dietitian whom he met in college, and they moved to San Diego, where she was employed at the county hospital, and he became a pachyderm specialist at the world-famous San Diego Zoo.

And so—life radically changed for the antelope of the Serengeti; it was the dawning of a new age. Never again would they let lions or other predators disturb their happy peace. As mentioned earlier, Bundy's original proposals were lame and dysfunctional, but from those blueprints, the antelope created clever ways as a team to catch lions, usually by baiting them with their imperiled youngsters and then sneaking up from behind with carefully sharpened antlers and impaling them before they had a chance to fight.

In order to better orchestrate their efforts, the antelope named one another. The first two to be named were a cute couple, Buck and Doe. They were given those names because it was what Bundy had called them, but in truth the names were just titles of convenience and Bundy would have addressed them all as "Buck" or "Doe" if he had needed to communicate with them individually. The single antelope the reader shall be concerned with henceforth is Harvey. Harvey was an easygoing antelope who typically followed the crowd but always wished he could rise up and be a leader among antelope. Harvey was best friends with Buck and usually hung around with him, going where Buck went and doing what Buck did.

Harvey was proud to be Buck's friend. Buck was a hard worker and team leader, and the others looked up to him, but, as with all leaders, he had a sense of entitlement about him. He worked hard and felt that he must be allowed to play hard. He considered himself a handsome male of great and irresistible virility to whom life had given a free pass to grab all the gusto he craved. Harvey egged Buck on in those feelings because he knew that any great rewards Buck received would trickle down to him. Over time, Harvey noticed a change in Buck that intimidated him though he didn't have the courage to stand up to his friend. The daily stress of Buck's efforts created a stronger-than-average sex drive, and he complained to Harvey about his frustrations.

"Doe," he said, referring to his wife, "is not willing to

put out for me in the sack." Since Doe was the mother of his two kids, Bernie and Liza, Buck didn't want to push the issue with her. "I'm afraid it would alienate her and the children," he explained. Instead, one day he espied a fair young damsel named Clarissa. She was a luscious little creature who had just reached puberty.

"She's ripe for the picking," Buck said as he and Harvey stalked her from behind some bushes. Harvey loved Buck's clever little metaphors like "ripe for the picking"; they represented a creative genius unknown in the antelope kingdom.

Over a period of weeks, Buck kept his eye on the fawn, carefully studying her daily habits. One evening after a hard day's work, Buck and Harvey cornered Clarissa, who was grazing behind a tree. At the opportune moment, they tackled and raped her. It was a grotesque and messy scene. There was screaming—the horrid screams of an antelope in pain—along with bodily fluids on display. The other antelope could hear Clarissa's cries but were too afraid to intervene.

The adrenalin-pumped act of rape was so exhilarating and transcendental to Buck that—out of the same predatory instinct he had awakened while trapping lions—he finished the ugly Clarissa business by gutting the pretty fawn and leaving her bloody carcass on the ground. As he walked away, he glanced back at her limp body a couple of times and growled in a strange and intense state of arousal. Harvey was not so enthused by the situation but was too intimidated to state his objections.

Among the first responders on the bloody scene was Clarissa's father, Francis Patrick. As can be imagined, he was enraged by the loss and mutilation of his daughter. It was one thing for a girl to be tracked down by the barbaric lions, but to have one's own comrades do such a dirty deed demanded immediate retribution.

After some cajoling, Francis convinced a posse of other antelope that an act this gruesome could deserve only the highest punishment.

That evening, while Buck was alone, slothing about behind some bushes and licking Clarissa's blood off his hooves, he was suddenly surrounded by a group of his peers. He tried to get up and run but was immediately tackled by two bucks while Francis Patrick, after making a hearty scream, drove forth and jabbed two of his freshly sharpened antlers into Buck's heart. Buck whimpered and whined to the great satisfaction of the other antelope and then gave his last gasp while his head dropped down on the ground.

"Let this be a lesson," Francis said as all the other antelope sat before him at a camp meeting, "to any and all recalcitrant antelope, that acts of violence amongst the herd will not be tolerated."

Francis Patrick was immediately named sheriff, and his first order of business was to banish Buck's cohort, Harvey, from the herd. Francis wanted to execute him, but Harvey's pleas about not wanting to actually injure Clarissa won the sympathy of other "old-boy" conservatives who felt that perhaps rape was an honest antelope's fun.

Shamefully exiled, Harvey moved on to another herd to which he provided an impressive résumé and a hard-told sob story about the brutality of Francis Patrick and his entire collective of fascists.

Harvey's stories instilled deep fear into his new friends, and they soon looked upon the original herd with great skepticism and dread. Those savages, they would exclaim, were worse than the lions as they had been given a trust as brothers and sisters and then betrayed that trust by killing an antelope and banishing another.

An ambush was arranged to capture a random member of the now-enemy herd. Perfectly executed, the enemy buck was then brutally disemboweled and left on the plains as a message to Francis Patrick and his cronies that such acts of violence would not be tolerated among the other tribes.

Francis Patrick immediately called a war council; it was the first of its kind, and his tribe was organized for an attack out on the Serengeti. Both sides held long meetings in which they sketched attack strategies on the dirt, using rocks to simulate battle formations as they designed creative tactics to outwit their enemy. Harvey's entire village, bucks and does, joined in to brainstorm how best to take down Francis Patrick's evil empire. After the meeting adjourned, a curfew and quarantine were established to ensure that no spies would sneak off and give away their strategy.

Elephants, giraffes, and rhinoceroses came out as spectators and lined the two sides of the savanna as the antelope tribes fought an intense battle for domination. The battle was long and brutal. There were bodies flung high into the air like they were shot from cannons while the crazed scream from massive charges echoed across the African wilderness. As with all civil wars, this one ended with a blood-red field of corpses all piled on top of one another, with the victorious leader climbing up onto the largest mountain of dead flesh and declaring his supreme power—praising God and Lord Jesus for once again supporting the righteous and humble over the wretched and arrogant.

In the end, Harvey's tribe triumphed—fear is the greatest motivator—and he was rewarded with the title Emperor of the Serengeti.

Harvey's first ironic order of business was to set up prison camps for recalcitrant antelope as well as any and all potential political foes. To ensure that there would be no challenge to his rule, he expanded his kingdom out to a very broad buffer zone and made sure to reward loyalty by creating a new class of wealthy landowners and promising the poorer of the herds that one day, if they worked hard, they too would partake in the wealth of the nation.

Over the years there was widespread poverty, occasional class battles, and a fair amount of malfeasance, but ultimately the antelope worked hard and actually created an industry out of killing lions and other predators.

Rabbits and smaller animals sometimes hired out the antelope for protection, but it was always a sketchy alliance because rabbits themselves were quite tasty, so it was hard to hold fast to contracts.

Despite the daily struggles to make ends meet and a regular fear of both criminal violence and police abuse, it was a decent life for the average antelope on the Serengeti. They soon forgot about their primitive past and became fully adapted to a life of industry and productive growth.

Meanwhile, back in San Diego County, Bundy McPherson and his lovely wife put a large chunk of their savings into lucrative mutual funds that netted them a handsome annual allowance, allowing them to purchase a time-share on Vancouver Island, where they traveled every August with their three darling children. The wildlife in British Columbia was plentiful, and Bundy made many friends.

THE DURSCHLAG TWINS

I swerved my car to the left, just narrowly avoiding the Durschlag twins. Those little girls were too much. Seriously, they had the run of the neighborhood. It was as if every single property and every object that wasn't tied down belonged to them. I screeched to a halt, and of course, they started crying in unison. The blonde one began hitting her head with her fist, and I had to reach over and grab her hand, causing the red-haired one to cry louder. Their mother, Doris, had dyed the twins' hair so she could tell them apart, but I still couldn't tell one from the other.

When the dust settled, it turned out they were playing with their little dolls. The twins each had identical twin daughters—grotesque rag dolls—all named Princess. According to the red-headed one, the four dolls had raced out into the street, and she and her sister followed after to rescue them just as I was coming over the hill. I nearly flattened the girls and their little rag toys.

Doris Durschlag came running out of the house in terror. She grabbed her little angels and yelled at me, calling me a reckless menace to the neighborhood. I was, in her words, driving at a madman's clip—in reality, almost fifteen miles per hour. Any slower and I might as well have pulled out a leash and walked my car home.

My personal issue with the twins went back a ways to when I came home from a morning golf game and found them in my front yard: One of them stood screaming while the other lay drowning in my sprinkler. I'm not exaggerating; she was flailing her arms, lying in a pool of water that the two of them had created by turning the sprinkler upside down. I called the fire department on my cell phone—which was a bit of an overreaction as it turned out—while racing to the rescue. I turned the hose off and grabbed the drowning redhead, who, after a few healthy smacks on the back, coughed the water up out of her lungs. It was a scene that got the attention of the Hitchenses, my neighbors from across the street, who made a series of frantic telephone calls before they came rushing out to help. Doris Durschlag was one of the phone recipients, and by the time she raced down the street, the fire department was approaching from the other direction. A police car was in close tow with its sirens blaring.

"What did you do to my children?" she yelled as she ran and scooped them up. The girls had calmed down but started crying again when they realized they were in the middle of a bona fide scene and it was their turn to shine. Doris called out to the cop as he stepped out of his squad car.

"Arrest him," she said, pointing to me. "He tried to drown my babies!"

Meanwhile, two firemen were trying to pry the nearly drowned girl from Doris's clutches so they could check her vitals. When the police officer approached, I explained I had been on the golf course since six that morning and pointed to my car, which was only partially pulled into the driveway with the driver's side door still open.

Everybody but Doris believed me.

As time went by, the goofy-faced little Durschlags developed a reputation for wandering the neighborhood like doped-up raccoons. They even went so far as to jump, unattended, on the Freiberg family's trampoline until, after fifteen minutes, the two of them did a seat drop together and went ripping through the canvas bed onto the hard ground, banging their collective asses. Even though they were only marginally in pain, they had been trained by their mother to bellow a shrill scream of terror whenever they were in trouble, which brought all the neighbors out of their homes and over to the Freibergs' backyard, and then, of course, someone called the cops. When Rob and Sheila Freiberg came home from an early matinee, there were flashing police lights out front and a crowd milling around their backyard as Doris Durschlag, clutching her two innocent babes, pointed at the Freibergs and yelled, "Killers!"

And now, on Draeger Street, it was my turn again to be the scapegoat.

"I'll have you locked behind bars for the rest of your natural life, you child endangerer!" Doris was screaming like a maniac, causing the Bobbsey Twins to start wailing loud enough to deserve one of those TV cartoon close-ups of their wide-open mouths revealing vibrating tonsils.

People were coming out onto their front porches and lawns to study the commotion. I would have thought that after nine years with these children, they would all have just assumed it was more Durschlag idiocy, but I guess there was always the fear that the kids might do something lethal on their property, à la the sprinkler incident at my house or the trampoline business at the Freibergs'.

"Look here, Doris. They ran in front of my car like frightened badgers."

"My children would do no such thing." She looked at them. "Would you?"

The blonde one started crying, holding up her twin rag dolls with one hand while pointing at me with the other.

Several of the neighbors had become interested in our exchange and had crept closer so they could hear the conversation. This was a chance for me to plead my case.

"What kind of mother lets her children play in the busy streets of the suburbs? Especially when they're obviously challenged."

That was a bad call. While I had her dead to rights on the playing in the streets point, I killed it when I brought up the pink elephant (or whatever you call it) about being "challenged." Everybody knew her children were missing a few pieces of mental machinery, but nobody dared say anything. I mean, it's not like they were mentally disabled or autistic or anything that would elicit support or sympathy; they were just peculiar in a *Children of the Corn* sort of way.

"You will regret those words, mister!" I had hit a nerve.

"Doris," I said. "Let's be adults about this. I have a right to drive home without kids running out in front of my car chasing rag dolls."

The redheaded one screamed, "They're not rag dolls; they're our children," and she started to cry some more.

"Do you see what you've done? You are a sick man," Doris yelled. The crowd was now growing on the sidewalk across the street. Doris looked around at the rubberneckers, none of whom were coming to her rescue. "You're all sick, every last one of you!" She was screaming hysterically like Blanche in *A Streetcar Named Desire*.

The blonde twin came to her rescue. "Mommy, it's OK. Our children made it!" She held up her two dolls. "We saved them from the bad driver."

"You haven't saved them, darling. You don't know." She pointed at me. "He'll keep coming. He'll always keep coming until he kills every last one of us." She looked around at the neighbors out on their front lawns and sidewalk. "And you don't care. None of you care!"

All of a sudden a police car appeared from around the corner. As soon as Doris saw it, she started waving at it madly. "Now you'll see!" she said.

The cop pulled over, looking bored and reluctant. He slammed the gearshift on his steering wheel into park and picked up his radio, probably to announce his location to the dispatcher. He stepped out of the car to the sound of Doris Durschlag yelling, "Arrest this man. He tried to kill my daughters!"

The redheaded twin yelled, "He tried to kill our daughters too," and she held up the rag dolls again.

"What exactly happened here?"

"What happened," I said, "was that I was driving home, down Draeger Street, at a safe speed"—I enunciated "safe" as I looked over at Doris—"when I saw a bunch of objects fly out into the street, and then these little imps came chasing after them, causing me to hit the brakes at the last minute."

The cop looked at Doris. "Where were you when all this happened?"

She pointed back at the house. "I was on the front porch, dutifully watching my children, and had just called them to come away from the street because I could hear this maniac with a revved engine a block away. This man was driving so fast it's a miracle my children were able to escape death."

"That's a damn lie!" I yelled.

"Please watch your language around my children."

"Sir," said the cop, "I'm going to have to ask you to tone it down, please."

I looked at the twins. "I'm sorry, girls." Of course the blonde one instantly started crying again.

"So how fast were you going, anyway?"

"No more than fifteen miles an hour. Believe me, sir. I live here. I know that there are children. Sometimes they play catch and a ball gets away. But this . . . this was deliberate."

"Deliberate?"

"Yes. Those children threw their dolls into the street because a car was coming and then ran out to grab them."

Now both of the twins were crying. The cop looked at me funny, as if maybe I was the one who was crazy. I looked across the street at the people on the sidewalk, but all were slowly starting to disperse, like they didn't want to get dragged into anything that included law enforcement.

I yelled at them, "Oh, come on!" The neighbors stopped to look at me as they were walking back into their homes. "Someone back me up." I yelled. "These kids are constant trouble!"

I looked back at the cop. "You," I said. "You must have reports on these kids; they're all over the neighborhood jumping people's fences like squirrels."

"Sir, what I see here is a tragedy averted. I'm not saying you were driving recklessly, and I'm not saying these kids were playing recklessly. I'm saying it's just one of those things. Now, let's face it. It's an act of grace for everybody involved that nobody got hurt."

He squatted down in front of the twins. "You two are very lucky to have children of your own," he said as he brushed one of the Durschlag's bangs out of her eyes. He looked at the other one. "My wife and I both love kids; wish we had some—maybe we will one day.

"Kids, it would be as horrible a day as ever could be imagined if two sweet girls like you . . . or your daughters," he said, nodding to the rag dolls, "ever got struck by a vehicle. I beg of you, little darlings, please look both ways before you run out into the street. Promise me this, will you, please? Promise Officer Ferguson that you'll never run into the street until you've looked both ways."

The two girls smiled. "We promise," they said in unison, and then the blonde one held up her two rag dolls and added, "They promise too."

Officer Ferguson had a tear in his eye as he looked up at me, standing there watching this pitiful little reenactment of a pedestrian safety film. "What do you think?" he asked me. "Will they ever run into the street again?"

What the hell could I possibly say?

"No, I think they understand the safety risks now, officer."

It was as unsatisfactory a moment as I could imagine, but then the blonde twin came and grabbed my left leg and hugged it. Then the redhead grabbed the other. The cop watched this as he stood up, and the tears began trickling down his cheeks. I looked over at Doris Durschlag, but she was not at all moved.

"Girls!" she barked. "It's time to go inside and let this nice policeman get back to catching criminals." They let go of my legs and waved goodbye to the two of us and followed their mother into the house.

Officer Ferguson looked at me and smiled. "Kids. They're so darn cute! Treat 'em right, and you got friends for life." He patted me on the back and walked over to his squad car and got inside. I walked over to my car, which was parked in the middle of the street, and I got in and drove home.

The next morning when I stepped out my front door, I found the little Durschlag twins walking up my lawn waving the morning paper as they carried it up to my front porch.

THORNCHILD

Delores spun around as she held her cell phone to her ear. She always did that—it was adorable. She got *so* into her conversations. And it wasn't just on the phone; she was like that at home and at restaurants and bars. It wasn't like she spun around while in direct conversation with you, but there was an active listening thing going on that just made George crave her in a big way.

Delores was talking to her sister, Carmen, on the phone as she stood in line at the pastry shop. She said Carmen's name twice is how George knew. He sat waiting for her at a table with his croissant and a can of Dr Pepper. Normally, George would have stood up and gone over and hugged her before she even got to the line at the counter, but she had the phone to her ear when she walked in. When he started to get up, she waved him off while she chatted it up with Carmen.

"Have you been inside the place?" she was asking. Her voice was loud, and George could hear her above the din of the other coffee shop-type conversation.

"It was gorgeous!" she said. "They have a fireplace in there. You could *literally* walk into it like a cave."

He knew she was talking about this estate she had just visited down south of here a couple of weeks ago. She said it blew her away. She was like that. She was always finding things to do that blew her away.

George watched her shut off the phone as she approached the counter and ordered her latte and croissant. When she came over, he stood up, and after she put her cup and plate down on the table, she gave him a hug and a kiss.

She looked down at the table and saw the can of Dr Pepper. She shook her head and grimaced.

"Caffeine," George said. "Just like coffee." She shook her head again. It was an old story. She referred to it as his final clinging to the "safety" of his old ways.

"We'll work on that," she said. She sat down. "So we're going today, George."

"Today? Where are we going, sweetie?"

"We're going down to the Thornchild estate."

"That's a two-hour drive, baby. Are you sure?" George didn't want her to be sure because he had hoped they would just lounge around or maybe go out to the lake with some deli sandwiches or something. But when Delores got something in her mind, it was pretty much a lock.

"Georgie, I can't let you live another minute in this world without you seeing the Thornchild estate. It's the most magnificent monument to mankind—heaven on earth."

Delores also had a penchant for hyperbole.

"Don't forget, the two-hour drive is *each way*, honey," I said.

"It'll go by so fast. You'll see."

Delores didn't waste time when there were things she wanted George to do. They munched down their croissants at an unhealthy pace. She had a way of doing it with grace though. She even licked the butter-soaked crumbs off her fingers delicately, like she was pruning a rose bush or something.

George, on the other hand, had to rush to keep up with her, and it created the impression of clumsiness. For the record, George wasn't clumsy; he'd been a decent athlete in high school and could still, at thirty-four years old, touch his toes without bending his knees. At least he assumed he could—George hadn't tried it in the year since Delores and he had gotten together. Still, his own personal grace factor was diminished greatly in the presence of such beauty and facility. But when you've got Delores on your arm, he figured, why would you still need to look like a shining knight to the rest of the world?

The drive down to Carlsberg was the usual joy ride of giggles and great tunes. Delores brought a new CD anthology of Van Morrison songs. It's a funny thing about Van Morrison. George's parents listened to him. In fact, they fell in love over the gentle crooning of "Tupelo Honey," so even though he didn't really know much about him, Van Morrison had a soft spot in George's heart. Delores knew about him. She knew about everything. She knew '60s rock and '30s swing and hip-hop; you go ahead and name it—she knew it.

"You have such great taste in music, honey," George said as he watched her hug the highway with the steering wheel.

"You're getting there," she said. "You're learning all the

good stuff, little by little. I can tell."

"You'll always be my master, sweetheart."

"Aww."

They took the Willow Canyon exit off the interstate and circled around to an underpass beneath the highway. She turned onto a long road that started to curve into beautiful countryside between two mountains.

"What a blissed-out place for somebody to live," George said.

"Oh, you just wait. It's beyond your wildest imagination."

They traveled on along a stretch of flora that grew in front of a half-mile of barbed wire fence until they got to the gravel entrance. The driveway passed through an open gate marked by two marble cherubim and led toward a massive lawn of fresh, carefully cut grass. There was a small gatehouse about a quarter of the way into the front of the estate grounds where a man with a cartoonish, Pluto-like face directed them to stop.

Delores opened her window, and a spray of hot air blew into the car. The air conditioning had hidden the fact that it was about twenty degrees warmer downstate.

"Do you have reservations?" the man asked.

"No. I was told we didn't need them on Tuesdays. It's the day of grace, you know."

"I'm just asking." He stuck his head partway into the car. "Just the two of you?"

"Yes," said Delores.

"That'll be eighty dollars, please."

George was stunned. They were dropping almost a hundred bucks at a moment's notice on a trip to nowhere. He pulled out his wallet and began forking out twenties.

Delores looked at him with loving, sympathetic eyes.

"I'm sorry, George. I should have warned you before we left. I wasn't thinking."

"No problem. This will be great."

Delores grabbed the bills from his hand and handed them to the gatekeeper, who counted them and then stepped into the booth and pulled out two clip-on ID badges for them.

"The parking lot's around the bend up there." He pointed to the road, which curved to the left past a grove of trees. "You can find a docent in the entrance to the main building. Enjoy your visit, folks."

"Thank you. You're so sweet," Delores said.

Delores drove down the road and veered to the left. The gatekeeper didn't need to give them directions because there was nowhere else to go. In front of them was a huge parking lot about two-thirds full. There were a handful of people walking around, including parents with their children, some being pushed in strollers. As they entered the parking area, George looked out his window, and there stood a humongous mansion. It was bigger than even the ones you see on TV—like a king's castle.

"Have you ever seen anything like this?" Delores asked.

"Pretty swanky digs," he said

"Wait until you see inside and out back."

The stone walkway to the entrance was surrounded by rose bushes and other pretty flowers; orchids and such—purple, yellow, and orange. The floral arrangement produced an intoxicating mix of aromas that no doubt had been carefully orchestrated by the gardeners.

Delores was wearing a little backpack that had a couple of bottles of water in it. She always did that when they went places; hydration was very important to her.

"They have a café here, George. It's adjacent to the first arboretum."

"Mmmm."

They were met at the entrance of the mansion by a silver-haired woman in a purple two-piece suit and white blouse. She held a stack of long rectangular cards printed on orange cardstock that told a brief history of the Thornchilds and their estate. It gave directions to points of interest and had a schedule of tour start times. The lady pointed them to an orientation desk where she suggested they go and sign in.

"I'd rather not do the formal tour unless you want to," Delores said. "I can take you around myself and show you the high points."

They went over and signed their names in the book. Delores then tugged George by the arm, and they stepped out of the huge front hallway with its high ceilings and crystal chandeliers and into a sitting-type room with dark-wood-paneled walls. She pointed to the corner of the room and said, "That's the bathroom if you need to go."

"What, the corner?"

"No, silly."

All of a sudden the wood seemed to open, and a man stepped out. Behind the door George could see the corner of a porcelain sink and white square tiles on the wall of the little bathroom. Delores looked at him and laughed.

"I'm OK," he said.

She led him through the back exit of the sitting room and through a dark hallway that was off the beaten trail.

"I found a shortcut," she said.

She was always finding things. It didn't seem like a shortcut though. It just seemed like a narrow side storeroom with a bunch of empty boxes. As they walked through it, they passed the back entrance to the kitchen. George peered in—it was huge.

"We'll check the kitchen out on the way back," she said as she tugged on his shirt again.

They found their way to a back door. The paint on the door was pealing, and it had four windowpanes on the upper half. Delores opened it and ushered George outside. They came out through a break in some bushes. On the shaded grass in front of them, children were playing on a rope swing hanging from a huge tree.

"Don't you love kids?" she said.

"Yeah."

The question was rhetorical. Kids had become a big subject for the two of them. They had now been seeing each other for over a year, they were both in their midthirties, and marriage and children had flooded her imagination. George hadn't totally bought into the idea, but his deep need for Delores told him that he would be a fool to not do whatever she wanted and risk losing her.

Delores walked up to the girl and boy. The girl had a pink ribbon in her hair that matched her pink-and-white dress. She was pushing the boy, who was sitting on the square, wooden seat that hung from a tree branch. The boy was complaining because the girl was pushing him too high and too close to the tree. The whole scene seemed like a pastel drawing of heaven that you'd see inside one of those Jehovah's Witness pamphlets.

"Careful, honey," Delores said. "You don't want your brother to scrape himself."

The girl stopped pushing him and looked up at Delores. "How did you know he was my brother?"

"Oh, brothers and sisters have a special little relationship with one another. It's written all over your faces."

The girl smiled as the boy urged her to push him some more.

"Don't you love kids?" Delores said as she grabbed George's hand.

She steered him away from the children and toward the marble steps that led to a magnificent ocean of gardens that seemed to stretch out several hundred yards toward the foot of the mountains. Beyond the steps was a concrete path—square slabs pressed into the green lawn—that ended at a long, narrow pool with a fountain in the middle.

Delores and George walked along the path until they reached the wide deck surrounding the pool. He walked over to the water and looked down inside.

"No goldfish," he said.

"No, no. This is a swimming pool, George. See how it gets deep around the middle where the fountain is and has steps on both sides?"

"I don't smell any chlorine."

"I don't think they want the visitors swimming."

"Huh."

"They have gardens dedicated to every kind of flower imaginable." She pointed to a passage through the bushes that ran along the backside of the pool area. "The rose garden is right back here."

They walked through the opening and into a vast, lush sea of roses. There were pinks and violets and whites with red trim. The garden smelled like heaven.

"This smells like heaven," Delores said.

George nodded his head, but the odor was overwhelming, and he stopped. He felt like he might need to sit down and looked around for a bench. There were none in eyeshot, but he noticed what looked like a chapel at the far end of the garden.

"Is that a chapel?" he asked.

"Yeah, it's weird. I've never heard of anyone having their own private chapel on their property."

George regained his composure, and they continued their turn through the garden. The walk was almost Victorian. George felt myself harnessed deep within Delores's world but had to hold his hands over his nose not to be intoxicated by the sharp smell of roses. It was like a thorn jabbing him in his nasal cavity.

"Are you all right?" Delores asked.

"It's nothing. I'm just a little nauseous."

"Oh, George, don't get sick. There's so much I want to show you. It's a wonderland. Actually, we could explore this place for eternity and never come to the end of it."

Suddenly George began to keel over involuntarily "I think I'm going to get sick."

"Oh, George. Please, let me get help."

The next thing he knew, he was on the ground holding his stomach. He felt like he was in a life-and-death struggle. His arms and chest were constricting, and his stomach was in razor-sharp turmoil like he had been poisoned. He was desperate to flush it out.

"Dr Pepper," George said without thinking. "Go to that café and get me a Dr Pepper. That's all I need; I swear."

"George, you know what's in that. That's the worst thing for you." She pulled out a water bottle and handed it to him. "This will help you."

"No, it'll kill me. Please, go get me a Dr Pepper. Hurry."

Delores typically didn't back down when she knew she was right, but the forcefulness of George's voice knocked her into an obedient trance. She walked quickly back toward the mansion, and George could feel some of the pressure release, so he started to get up. He was still wobbly but felt an overwhelming attraction to the chapel at the far end of the rose garden. He began staggering down an aisle of roses past a happy couple who looked at him in shock. It was as if they didn't know whether to offer him help or run for cover. He stumbled past them faster than they could make a decision.

The chapel was very small. There were steps leading up to the door under an A-framed roof held up by two round, wooden pillars. George pushed open the door, and it was empty inside save for two rows of pews with an aisle in the middle. At the front there was a little pulpit on a wooden riser. Behind the pulpit, there was a white cross hanging on the center of the wall and stained-glass windows on either side. In the glass there were pictures—violent biblical scenes of Daniel being fed to lions and Jesus falling in one of the Stations of the Cross.

Suddenly, George felt a deep and embedded sense of ease.

He sat at a pew and began breathing deeply. It seemed that with each breath, a sense of certainty washed over his body. He smiled dreamily as he sat looking at the colored windows. The sun was in such a position that some of the colors reflected off of his hands as he sat comfortably waiting. Waiting for what he did not know.

After about ten minutes, George got up and walked to the door and stepped outside the chapel. He looked to the far end of the rose garden and saw Delores. She looked up at him and waved. He couldn't hear her, but she seemed to be mouthing the words, "There you are!" As she waved, the cramps and sickness began to fill his stomach again, and he rushed back into the chapel and slammed the door.

He walked up the aisle and stopped directly in front of the pulpit, where he fell on his knees and started to pray.

"Oh, God. Please, God, get me the hell out of here. I can't stand it anymore!"

As he stood up, the door to the chapel opened, and Delores stepped inside.

"George, what are you doing?"

He didn't say anything. She walked over to him with the can of Dr Pepper, and he grabbed it from her and sat down at the pew. He took a couple of big gulps. It was delicious; it washed out all the sickness inside of him. He continued to sit silently on the bench as Delores stared at him.

Finally he said, "Delores, I think we have some things to talk about."

ELOI REDUCTION

"They're still sorting things out," the KTLA newscaster said with a microphone in hand, "but it's safe to say this is the most heinous act of violence and depravity LA has ever seen." Then she added, "And that's saying a lot." She was standing out on the sidewalk in a bath of bright lights with a crowd of onlookers roped off on either side of her.

Sergeant Adams stood inside the warehouse looking at the huge vat and elaborate factory equipment in disbelief. Adams had always suspected something was wrong—hell, everybody did. Whenever he'd patrol the boulevard with other officers, it seemed the conversation would always turn to one question: "Where the hell do they come from?"

"They" referred to the long line of immaculate, nubile women and androgynous teenage boys waiting to get into the private rave at the giant nameless warehouse on Hollywood Boulevard, a block and a half past Gower Street. There was never a marquee out front, or flyers, or any kind of public listings for the parties except on a handful of obscure websites.

Adams stood on the floor of the warehouse with Lieutenant Collins, who was among the first responders to the scene.

Collins had been onsite for several hours while a second team back at headquarters interviewed suspects and put together all the pieces. He explained the situation to Adams—his voice distorted by a pair of nose plugs he was wearing. They were the rubber kind that swimmers used to wear. Adams himself didn't notice any stench and figured the room must have aired out.

"If it wasn't for our favorite street drunk, Red Pupkin," Collins said, "we'd never have stumbled onto this mess."

As they talked, a police team lifted up the corrugated metal doors of the two loading entrances, and a bright orange glow flooded the warehouse from the halogen streetlights outside. Several television reporters were standing out front with the growing crowd, which was kept behind yellow police tape. News vans with round, microwave antennas protruding up to the sky were double-parked on the boulevard. The antennas towered over the milling throng out on the curb. An aisle had been opened up amid the crowd so that policemen and other officials could get in and out of the warehouse without incident.

"So that goofy son of a bitch Pupkin discovered this whole thing?" Adams asked.

"Sort of. It was Officer Jacobsen who followed him in here; they both barely made it out alive. If Jacobsen wasn't such a trigger-happy asshole, the two of them would be dead. Apparently, security for this operation was intense."

"Where's Jacobsen now?"

"Oh, you won't be seeing him for a while. Aside from the leave he has to take for the shootings, he's totally freaked out by the whole deal."

"How's Pupkin handling it?"

"Ha! He's been through so many DT bouts, he probably thinks this was just another hallucination."

Adams took another glance around the warehouse where crowds of cops, FBI agents, and forensic experts were talking and pointing.

"So what exactly happened and how does Red fit in, for Chrissakes?"

"Well, you know how Red likes to hound the young girls in the rave lines up and down Hollywood Boulevard. Since he's generally broke, his cruising only lasts long enough for a bouncer to kick the shit out of him. Either that, or somebody calls the cops and we cart him away."

Adams smiled. Red Pupkin was a major pain in the ass for the entire precinct, but most of the cops liked him anyway. He even served as an informant occasionally, despite his unreliability.

"Apparently Pupkin's aunt died, and he came into about fifty grand," the lieutenant continued.

"Yeah, I heard." Adams laughed. "He's been making a big hit in the bars on Sunset since he got rich."

Collins laughed. "He tried to get a room over at the El Capitan two nights ago and made a scene until they threw him out."

"Who the fuck comes into a shitload of money and then stays at the El Capitan?"

"Well, Red does or tries to at least. Anyway, last night, rather than doing his usual ritual of buying a pint of gin and hitting on the girls in the lines outside the clubs, he comes directly here to the Morlock Club and—"

"*That's* what they call this thing? The *Morlock* Club?"

"Pretty fitting, isn't it?"

"Wow. They were certainly hiding in plain sight, weren't they?"

"Yeah, so Red decides to get in line with the girls. He's all bathed up and dressed in brand-new clothes, so nobody really notices him."

Adams had a thought. "Hey, I don't get it. Something this obvious—how come nobody ever reported this place to the authorities?"

"They don't let older people inside except for the men who work here. The crew will dress up and act as decoys or ringers and wait in line with the rest of the crowd. They'll be ushered through the door along with all the girls just to make the place look legit and then go back out and stand in line again."

As the two officers were talking, four beautiful young blondes, wrapped only in blankets, were escorted past them by a short, tough female cop. A bunch of camera flashes went off among the crowd at the gate, and a few reporters could be heard calling out to the police escort to turn the girls over to them for a quick interview.

Collins turned to the reporters and yelled, "Heartless bastards!" It was not loud enough to cut through the noise but seemed to make him feel better as he turned back to Sergeant Adams.

"Well, you know how the whole club scene goes. Guys stand in line for hours, and then as they get up to the front, the bouncer will pick out a couple of them to come in and then either keep the others waiting or send them home."

"It's so stupid."

"Yeah, well this was the first time Red ever had money to actually attend something like this, and he was chomping at the bit to spend some quality time with all the young clubber chicks."

"Yeah, like he's going to make a big hit with the young ladies. He's either dribbling drunk or shaking like a Chihuahua."

"So when Pupkin gets up to the front of the line, he's holding a pint of Gilbey's in his hand—obviously a big no-no outside a nightclub—and the bouncer recognizes him and starts yelling, calling him all sorts of expletives. A redneck drunk from out of town is standing right behind Red and thinks the bouncer is talking to him and explodes. Meanwhile, Jacobsen and his new rookie partner, Finn, happen to be cruising by and notice Pupkin just as the altercation starts flaring up. They immediately pull over as the first fists start flying. They charge the front of the warehouse to break up the fight when Jacobsen notices Red dashing into the club. He sees that Finn's got the fight under control, so he rushes through the door after Red while the bouncer's screaming at him, 'You can't go in there!'

"It's pretty dark inside, but Jacobsen's able to make out a bunch of young chicks and a few boys standing in a waiting area with gags around their mouths. Apparently they get the attendees to put the gags on willingly, like it's part of an elaborate game, and since everybody's doing it, they assume it's safe.

"As his eyes get better adjusted, Jacobsen sees a couple of big, burly security-type guys chasing Red and, thinking he's being of assistance, he runs after Pupkin too. One of the security dudes sees him and freaks. He grabs an iron bar that's part of the equipment and begins wailing on Jacobsen." Collins pantomimed with his arms like he was beating on somebody.

"Hell," he continued, "you know how quick Jacobsen is though. Before the dude could possibly knock him out, he grabs his gun and starts firing every which way. The next thing you know, there are five wounded men lying on the warehouse floor. A bunch of others, including Red, go tearing out the door into the night. Jacobsen gets on the radio and announces he's under attack, and that's how the squad got here."

Adams looked around at the equipment, shaking his head as he tried to put some kind of story to the madness.

"God," he said, "the level of sexual perversion in LA has really sunk to an all-time low."

"You're wrong there, sergeant."

"What do you mean? What are you talking about?"

"Sex had nothing to do with this, man. Do you even know what was happening here?"

"Only what I heard on the radio."

"Well, grab your vomit bag, and I'll give you a tour."

The lieutenant led Adams back out front to the main gate and pointed at a long row of black curtains on rolling rods that were now stashed behind wooden benches against the wall of the warehouse. "Those curtains were placed in two rows in front of the main entrance so that when the clientele came through the door, they couldn't see what was actually happening inside. There were benches set up in a waiting area in front of the first curtains where the girls and boys would sit until someone was ready to see them."

Adams shrugged his shoulders. "It sounds innocent enough. I guess that helped settle them down a little, huh?"

"Yeah, well, according to witnesses, the customers were told that they would get their picture taken as VIPs when they were escorted into the second area. As soon as one of the club workers was free, he would call a group in and snap a photo of them. They would then be seated on another bench behind the second set of curtains where they were informed that, as part of the deal of entering into the club, they would have to put gags over their mouths. It was like a game. Apparently, now and then, a chick would freak out and refuse to do it. She'd be escorted back outside."

"They let 'em leave? Wouldn't they tell all the others in line what was going on?"

"Sure, but that just made most of the people in line more excited. The idea that hundreds of women were all letting themselves be gagged before they could enter a rave seemed like a wonderful novelty. One of the survivors said it 'sounded like a party for the ages.'"

"God, kids have changed since I was a teenager."

"Not really, sergeant. There's always been a handful of chicks from every town that run off to Hollywood so they can be part of something like this. Boys too."

"I guess."

"Well, so what the customers didn't know was that as soon as they were escorted past the second curtain there was a big burly security guy waiting who would grab their arms, pull them behind their back and handcuff them. They were then dragged over to that back wall," Collins pointed, "and shackled to that long pipe running along the floor." There were empty handcuffs and shackles attached to the pipe that ran along the cinderblock wall beneath worn-out posters of movie actors—Kathleen Turner in *Body Heat*, Kevin Spacey with the fourteen-year-old girl in *American Beauty*, and Marilyn Monroe with

Tony Curtis and Jack Lemmon dressed in drag in *Some Like It Hot*.

"This *is* beginning to make me sick," Adams said. "Fortunately I already know the worst part of the story, so I'm ready to hear this."

"No, you *don't* know the worst part of the story. I mean, yeah, it's obvious with the vat and cooking equipment what happened here, but it's even sicker than you can imagine."

"Go on."

"Well, as you probably heard, that huge vat was filled with boiling water."

"Good grief."

"The boys and girls were stripped down while chained to the wall, and a second photo was taken of them gagged and naked."

Adams gasped. "Oh Lord Jesus. Who the hell were these poor kids?"

"That's the thing, sarg. Like I was saying, this country is full of young, pretty gals and good-looking guys whose greatest fantasy is to make it big in Hollywood. Some are runaways. Others, well, their parents actually send them out here."

"OK, so these evil fucks boiled them alive. They didn't rape 'em first? As sick as that sounds, it just doesn't make sense to me."

"It's strictly business, man."

"*Business*? What the *fuck*?"

Collins escorted Adams over to the factory equipment. There was a crane over the giant vat.

"This, sergeant, is an assembly line. Once the bodies have been parboiled for approximately seven minutes, that crane reaches in, pulls the bodies out, and places them on a conveyer belt. The flesh has been boiled exactly to a point where it peels right off the bone like—"

Adams suddenly wrenched over but was able to stop himself from throwing up.

"I told you to bring your barf bag," Collins said.

"Fuck you. This is no joke."

"I was serious. So anyway, the bones, the organs, and the heads are all discarded down onto a long gutter along the floor over on the other side, and the boiled flesh is carried by the belt into this back section here."

The two cops walked beside the conveyor belt into a second large room separated by cheap drywall, where there were automated chopping machines next to an industrial oven. It reminded Adams of something the Mad Hatter or the Riddler would operate in the old *Batman* TV series.

"Here they get filleted, sautéed, and carried into that oven to broil for another six minutes."

Collins led Adams to the backside of the oven, where another conveyer belt led into a giant canning machine.

"So this is the craziest part. Hold on to your stomach. The cooked meat is then packed into tin cans. And you know those photographs they took of the customers out front?"

Adams was feeling faint and couldn't respond to Collins's question.

"Well," Collins said, "the images are uploaded into labeling software, and the machine wraps the label with their pictures right onto the can."

Adams suddenly noticed a huge stack of tin cans on the other side of the canning machine. He grabbed the side of the conveyer belt to keep from fainting.

"Here," Collins said, "take a look at this."

Collins took one of the cans off the stack wrapped in yellow police tape. He handed it to Adams, who barely held back weeping as he looked at the twenty-four-ounce can of meat. It read, "Morlock Brand Hollywood Stars & Starlets," and it had a picture of a pretty young blonde next to the brand name.

"Who the fuck would buy this?" Adams snapped.

"Are you kidding? We've already looked at the account logs. It's all the rage among Hollywood executives. One of the workers we talked to here said the execs throw wild parties and serve them for hors d'oeuvres. Apparently, it's also a popular party treat for US congressmen—*particularly* the gay-bashing conservatives from the South. Hell, that same worker told us it was a running joke among the bosses here that if you heard a congressman publicly complain about the moral depravity of Hollywood, he was probably one of Morlock's regular customers.

Adams had held back as best he could but finally burst into tears. Collins put his arm around him. "Let it out, sergeant," he said. "We all did the same thing at some point today. The worst part of it is, all the big shots who were buying the stuff will probably get off scot-free."

"How the fuck can they get away with it?"

"It's Hollywood and the United States Congress. They'll spin the story so fast. The next thing you know they'll be heroes."

"Shit, they'll probably make a blockbuster movie out of it."

"Yeah, yeah, you got it. And they'll drag another mass of tender young girls out here to play the parts."

"Jesus." Adams pulled a handkerchief out of his pocket and

began to dab his eyes and wipe his nose. Finally he said, "Hey, I gotta break away. I can't handle this."

"I understand. I wouldn't blame you if you hit a bar and had a drink, but remember, clock out and take your uniform off first."

Adams lowered his head and turned around, walking out to the main room past the chopping machine and across to the front entrance. As he stepped outside, he was bombarded by flashing camera lights and voices shouting pleas for a statement. He held up his hand and said, "I just got here. I know as much as you do."

"Aw, come on," said a reporter holding a mic to his face. "You gotta give us something."

"You goddamn media types are no more than grubby little rodents looking for filth you can feed your viewers!" Adams shot back. "Well, I'll give you something . . . digest this one. Your own fat-cat bosses and their slimy hacks in Washington are literally gobbling up America's youth. You guys in the news used to be America's last line of defense—now all your petty intrigue and gossip does nothing more than provide a nice subterfuge for the real crimes you ought to be covering."

Adams raised his fist like he was ready to deck the reporter who was questioning him when one of the officers at the gate grabbed him and held him back.

"Sarg, you don't want to be the story here. That's what they're looking for."

Adams dropped his fist and a couple of other officers stepped in front to cover him so he could make his exit. They escorted him into the crowd and then, in all the hubbub, he managed to escape to the other side of the street without notice.

That's what the whole goddamn country's looking for, he thought as he walked alone over to Gower Street. His chest was heaving and tears stung his eyes. *They all want someone to make 'em feel like victims so they don't have to face the monstrous crimes they perpetuate every day.*

He knew he had to keep moving. Turning down to Sunset, he wondered if he could ever walk far enough to get away from the horror of what he had just seen.

GEESE & GANDERS

The movie was awesome and left Otto satisfied that his second date with Claudia would prove to be the real thing – the path to true courtship. He was done with the Mickey Mouse one-night-stand stuff he'd experienced with other women. He had promised Claudia the movie wouldn't just be crashing cars and guts ripped open by bullets. Yeah, of course there was a little of that—men and women need to compromise—but there was a lot of thought to it as well. There was a deep sense of meaning in the movie that could be talked about by couples in cafés late into the evening. His last girlfriend always praised him for his generosity in their movie choices. He rarely put up much of a fight, but it was because Otto knew the vital importance of processing movie plotlines when developing a relationship—it was almost like they ran parallel to each other.

It was exactly this kind of thought-provoking conversation that Otto looked forward to as they settled into Starbucks across from the theater on Van Ness Avenue. Claudia ordered a latte, which was a good sign. It meant she had a desire to stay up late into the night. He followed suit but had a pump of caramel in his. They paid for their drinks separately, which

Otto figured was also good because it was her way of saying she would not be bought; they would unite on equal footing with equal passion for each other. And besides, he didn't have a lot of money anyway.

They found an empty table in the corner by two windows, one looking out onto Van Ness and the other onto a little alley along the side of the building. Cars were lined up in the alley at a Burger King drive-through. Just outside the coffee shop window, a teenage couple was in an old 1980s Mustang convertible and looked so happy. Otto remembered that simple joy. Twelve years prior, shortly after he got his driver's license, he took Carly Wilson on a date, and they drove through the Westlake In-N-Out Burger in Daly City after seeing *The Matrix Revolutions*. They sat together in the car in the parking lot, eating burgers and talking about how life really was a matrix and they were obviously somebody's pawn, but whose? That conversation landed him a year of love and companionship with Carly, until her parents sent her to a private boarding school down in Carmel for her senior year.

Four years in college and the ensuing effort to create a future for himself separated the Carly Wilson year from any later fulfilling relationships. His love life, it seemed, had been relegated to pickup bars with work buddies, which, though he did manage to make some okay friendships, never really brought him the kind of relationship he craved.

This particular evening's movie was a modern-day spy flick. It was the story of a double agent who sneaks secret data out of the Pentagon and gives it to a dangerous group of Maldivian cyberterrorists who threaten to hold the United States government hostage. While it was marketed as an action thriller, Otto thought it had a lot of depth and said much about trust and the values of right and wrong. Much of the top-secret data, which was to be made public by the terrorists, revealed that a private, international security firm had been hired by a secret White House intel group to torture and brainwash American prisoners in an Aleutian Islands prison camp. They were then turned into automaton soldiers and sent out into the world as a follow-up to drone attacks.

The underlying mission of the Maldivian terrorist group was to shed light on the plight of island nations being wiped out by rising oceans due to global warming. The Aleutian prison camps were a bit of a stretch, but the filmmakers justified everything pretty well. In a sense it was like *The Mouse That Roared*, but without the satire.

"You like caramel in your latte," Claudia said. "That's so cute!"

"My mom turned me on to caramel lattes when I was sixteen. We were down in San Diego visiting my uncle Seymour."

"I like San Diego. It's got nice beaches."

"I like beaches." Otto was excited that it was only their second date, and they had so quickly found common ground.

"So what did you think about the movie?" Claudia asked.

This was a tricky question because it could lead to irreversible political differences if not answered correctly. In a perfect world, Otto would hold off on his opinions until he heard Claudia's and then carefully wrap his opinions around hers. On the other hand, he had observed over the years that standing one's ground politically and philosophically was a great way to get laid. It seemed that women love to have sex with strong-minded men. The thing was, Otto wanted a long-term partner more than he wanted to just have sex.

"The movie was pretty cool," he said after a moment's pause. "I bet a lot of that stuff is true."

"What, concentration camps where felons are turned into elite military killers?"

"I don't know, but hell, you figure there's gotta be a lot of secret shit going on."

"So, do you think the Silver Fox was a hero or a traitor?"

Otto thought this was a question that should probably have been asked much later in the conversation. The Silver Fox was the name of the seventy-year-old spy who stole all the intelligence data and was trying to transmit it to the terror group that was based on a deserted island in the Indian Ocean. The data had all been downloaded onto a little memory stick to be smuggled out of the country because the Pentagon firewalls were impregnable and the NSA computers would freeze and analyze all electronic data that was transmitted off US soil.

"In the world of war and espionage," Otto said, "I don't think it's black and white—there are no real heroes or villains."

"Yeah, that's how I feel. But I guess the question is about trust."

"Yeah, trust. That's a heavy thing."

"Well, what would you do if, in order to be hired for a job you truly loved, you were required to make a vow to uphold confidentiality?"

"I guess it depends on what that confidentiality was."

"Well, of course you couldn't know until after you made

the vow."

"I don't think there's a job I'd ever want that would do crazy things like start a concentration camp in the Aleutian Islands."

"Me neither, but things change. Businesses grow and diversify."

"I guess it would depend on what the info was. But don't forget, in the movie the Silver Fox sold us out to terrorists."

"Yeah, but he didn't have a choice."

Otto realized as the conversation progressed that this was not the direction he wanted to go. There was no way he could maneuver the thought-provoking tension of this conversation toward his or her living room couch where they would snuggle and move toward the bedroom and a whole new level of conversation.

"I like your blouse. I meant to tell you that when I picked you up."

"Thank you. I love blue."

"It goes so nice with your blue eyes."

Claudia smiled demurely. This was the first time Otto had made a direct comment on Claudia's looks. She was attractive—her chestnut hair intensely accentuated the blue eyes and made them almost like a doorway to somewhere. In a sense they intimidated him. They were almost "dirty"—as in naughty.

He'd only seen eyes like that once before—at a Christmas party at work several years ago. There was a receptionist from a department two floors below who flirted with him next to the mistletoe through the whole party. They kissed discretely but passionately a couple of times with the obvious promise of sexual fulfillment. Her dirty eyes hid secret fetishes he was dying to uncover, but then she had a couple too many drinks and had to be carried out and put into a taxicab before he could get any contact information from her. It turned out she was only a temp and moved on before he had a chance to reconnect. He would have gone to great lengths to track her down, but her public drunkenness at the Christmas party made her a dangerous topic around the office, and you can't just drop into HR for things like that anyway.

The thing with Claudia was that, aside from the potential political landmines that stood before them by discussing the movie, those dirty eyes could present a problem as well. There was nothing wrong with marrying a "naughty" woman who liked to play nasty and hard, if that was the case, but if that aspect took center stage too soon, it might destroy the natural arc of the relationship that he really hoped would develop.

"You have pretty eyes too," Claudia said.

"Thank you. Brown's not quite as provocative as blue though."

"Provocative? How do you mean?"

What the hell did he mean? Sex? Otto looked down at his coffee cup. It was only caffeine, but he was starting to blither like a drunk. He thought about it.

"I mean provocative as in producing an emotion—an attraction."

"Mmmm."

"So why didn't he have a choice?" Otto asked.

"Excuse me?"

"The Silver Fox. You said he didn't have a choice."

"Oh." She took a sip from her latte. "Well, if he had tried to go anywhere in the US to reveal the information, he would have run the risk of not only being discredited but executed as a traitor."

"But why go anywhere? He took a loyalty oath to his country."

"Not to a country that tortures the disenfranchised and turns them into suicide killers overseas."

"That's true, but they weren't exactly disenfranchised. They were felons and drug addicts. I guess the question is, where do you draw the line? Are any oaths sacred?"

"Sure, by their very nature oaths are sacred. But you're forgetting something. The head of the program stated unequivocally that it was an honorable program, and he would never use child molesters, or, how did he put it, 'other low-life scum.'"

"Your point?"

"Well, by that very statement, he placed a moral bar on the quality of people he was enslaving. If it really was a penance thing, then the 'low-life scum'—the child molesters—would be the first ones out onto the front line. This was an out-and-out violation of human rights."

The naughtiness seemed to recede in Claudia's eyes as she expressed herself. She was no whore by any stretch. She was an intelligent and deeply thoughtful woman. The naughty eyes were for the darkened bedroom late at night, or maybe not so late but still for a private place.

They both took sips of their drink at the same time and then put them down awkwardly. Claudia giggled.

"So how's the caramel?" she asked.

"Delicious. They do it great here at Starbucks."

"It's funny how, since Starbucks has gotten so big, they've somehow become the enemy of the common people."

"The what?"

"You know, not literally, but in the public's eyes. Now they're just another big corporation that's scrutinized and accused of stealing opportunities from mom-and-pop businesses in local neighborhoods."

"Yeah, it must be rough being successful like that." Otto was not intending to be sarcastic, but a statement like that has no choice but to sound that way. Fortunately, Claudia laughed.

"You know," she said, "they're the perfect example of what we're talking about."

"How so?"

"Well, you go to work for them and you get bound to their corporate secrets. One day, as they grow, those secrets begin to be reshaped until you're bound to some horrid apocalyptic beast. Sort of like Google or Facebook."

"Exactly! All it takes is one guy in the planning and development department who proposes to put a Starbucks in Yemen or some other terror zone and then you're in line with the devil. The next thing you know, you're inviting some private security outfit like the one the Silver Fox worked for to keep you safe. Then you become the ideal spy machine for black ops overseas. In the meantime, you're getting lambasted on Fox News for being some pansy, "liberal" coffee shop while you're secretly smuggling arms to fascist groups in Syria.

"I wonder, do you suppose Starbucks is a major arms broker and intelligence center in the Middle East?"

Claudia laughed. "Are they even *in* the Middle East?"

"Oh fuck, Starbucks is *every*where!"

This was the critical and pivotal moment. It was imperative

that their conversation leave the realm of politics and international espionage and move on to bonding.

"Do you read much?" he asked.

"Sure, I like romance novels particularly. I bet you don't read much of that though."

"Not much." He laughed but then worried that he might be sending her the wrong signal. "But I like some romance movies," he said, "if they have a little humor to them."

"Me too. I love romcoms."

"Romcoms?"

"Romantic comedies."

"Oh yeah, me too! That's what I was talking about."

"We should definitely see one together."

"Yeah, totally!"

They were so close to the bedroom, Otto could hardly stand it. More importantly, though, was that they now had a pending date to see a romcom.

"This has been really nice," Claudia said.

"Yeah, I enjoy being with you."

"I like your mind, Otto. I like how you think."

"Really?"

"Yeah, most guys are just a firewall of unexamined agenda."

"Just like in the movie. Everybody jumps on the bandwagon without thought and assumes life is black and white."

"Exactly! That's the problem. Everybody thinks it's OK to differentiate their own personal trip from the big picture or vice versa."

"Any sense of meaning has been completely convoluted by power and greed." Suddenly Otto felt sophomoric. Of course, everything is convoluted by power and greed. Even a third-grader knows that.

"Everybody knows that," Claudia said, "and yet the same mistakes keep happening over and over, like somehow *this* time things will be different. Everybody pretends that habits don't create reality, that greed will solve the greed problem."

"So how does this fit into loyalty oaths?"

"I don't know. Maybe taking an oath like that comes with the assumption of basic moral obligations on the part of the business. The moment that gets compromised, the oath is rendered invalid."

"So, if I were a business, would you ever sign a loyalty oath with me?"

"That depends. Are you planning to diversify in the future?"

"Well, you can't really expect to know that until you sign the agreement, huh?"

"I guess not. I guess I'm obligated as long as there is mutual integrity."

They were both silent for nearly half a minute. Otto wondered if it was due to the awkwardness of his proposal—it was a little heavy a little fast—but surely she knew it was in jest. The real meaning of the silence had to be the strange microcosm of the big questions about loyalty and such.

"It's weird to think about it," she finally said, "when you put the question on a personal level. It makes the big issues have more clarity as well."

"Yeah. It's almost like what's good for the goose is good for the gander."

"Huh?"

"I don't know. It's like if you're expected to behave a certain way as an individual, why should it be different when you're bonded to something bigger."

Claudia started laughing. "Actually, I did understand," she said, "It just sounded so funny."

They were silent again. After a few moments, Claudia grabbed her latte and took a huge gulp.

"Hey," she said, "do you wanna get refills and come over to my place? I'm just up Van Ness on Clay Street."

"Yeah, that would be cool."

Claudia smiled and winked at him.

Otto felt like he had stepped into a new dimension. The invitation, the dirty eyes, the geese and ganders—all of it seemed to coalesce into the mist of a new and special journey.

SILENCIUM

"Everybody stop," Calvin yelled. "We're retreating to the library until the rain lets up."

There was a collective "Awww! But why?" from the rotten little campers who worshipped the hour they spent each day firing bullets everywhere but at the paper NRA targets, which were attached to a pair of wires approximately fifty feet away.

Though it was only a light sprinkle, Calvin knew that in the Midwest, torrential downpours could come in a flash, and the last thing he wanted was for a .22-caliber rifle to explode in some camper's face because Calvin was too stupid to pull the kids out of the rain. Even though he was reasonably sure that bullets couldn't randomly explode inside a rifle chamber, the moisture and humidity of the rain was intense, and he assumed he was showing common sense by pulling the kids away. He was also hopeful he would get some much-desired kudos from Brigadier General Carlson, the camp director, but it was one of those things where he'd rather have no praise than be blamed for some stupid kid's death.

Calvin earned the job as camp riflery counselor in the summer of '72 because he had been awarded a Bar 7 in marksmanship from the NRA at an overnight summer camp he had attended for five years. General Carlson couldn't find anybody else in the summer camp counselor market with riflery training, so Calvin got the job with little effort. He liked riflery; it quieted his restless, overly horny teenage mind and took his attention away from Debbie del Carlo and Susan Vincent, who were both away with their parents for the summer.

Debbie del Carlo was in Italy, and Calvin was sure some sexy Italian gentleman in a Ferrari would swoop her up, and he'd lose her forever. That would leave him to try his luck with Susan Vincent, who was only staying up in Lake Geneva, Wisconsin, for the summer. In a worst-case scenario, Susan might get banged once or twice by a drunken Wisconsin greaser dude, but Calvin would still have a shot at her when senior year started in September. It pissed him off terribly to think about how drunken greasers got to have all the fun with chicks while he had to hold down a stupid job counseling little rich snots at a summer camp in Lake Forest, Illinois. The upside of life was that Calvin had an OK pot connection and knew that, in the big picture, Susan would go for a freak much sooner than she'd settle in with a jock or a greaser. It was Debbie who presented complications.

All in all, though, he was happy to have a summer job rather than sitting around the house moping about chicks. The summer camp gig was important. It would provide him a solid base for job references as the course of his life moved forward. His brother's strong influence had convinced him to turn down an internship with the Mercantile Bank in Chicago, where their father was on the board, so this was the best he had. Plus, he was making enough money to save up for a brand-new Sansui receiver and Cerwin Vega speakers. Led Zeppelin records sounded best under those conditions.

Calvin had an older brother named David who was studying poli-sci at UCLA out in California—paradise, as Calvin understood it—and regularly sent him letters about the Vietnam War in which he explained that the bankers and arms builders were going to take over our country now that Nixon was sure to be reelected to a second term. Calvin worshipped David and read his letters over and over, and sometimes wondered if it was even worth his time to pursue a career or a girlfriend when the whole charade would soon come crashing down in revolution or a fascist dictatorship. How ironic it was that Calvin was working under the tutorship of General Carlson who had, over the past five years, steered the wealthy Lake Forest Summer Day Camp into a regimented boot camp for snot-nosed youth.

He called himself Brigadier General Carlson, but he wasn't really a general. He served as an NCO in World War II, missing D-day by several weeks but coming into Europe on a "second wave." He loved to tell those stories—to regale the summer campers with the heroics of his generation, which marched across France to Germany and drove Hitler to his grave. Given his druthers, General Carlson would have driven all the way across Poland and into Moscow to solve the Red problem as well.

Calvin enjoyed his stories and thought that the general was a decent enough guy—maybe even a hero like so many of his generation. But to Calvin, he was mostly just the man who signed his paycheck, rewarding him each week for managing the rifle range without incident.

"I want you all to stand at attention in a single line," Calvin said, "and then we'll do a right face and march across the soccer field and up to the library." Camp rules required that all the kids fall in line and march to their next destinations.

This particular group of ten-year-olds, the "Iroquois," was difficult for Calvin to handle. It was partly due to the fact that Richie, the son of Lake Forest Mayor Tobin, was one of the campers, and he was especially privileged and obnoxious.

As the kids began to march forward through the rain along the black cinder track that circled the wet soccer field, Richie broke rank, running up ahead to Calvin to protest the decision. He spoke with great philosophic precision for a fifth-grader.

"Calvin, I hope you understand that my father pays good money to this organization so that I can shoot a rifle every day. He's also a benefactor of Lake Forest Preparatory Summer Day Camp and could pull the plug on this joint with a single jot of the pen."

"Richie, I imagine your father loves you very much and would rather you be safe in the library than be dead on the rifle range."

"I think you're overreacting. I don't think you really know anything about rifles or riflery. Heck, we've never seen you shoot one."

"That's right," said Billy Connor, who then also broke rank, stopping in his tracks and causing the other kids to stop as well. Calvin was about to raise his voice and order the children back into single file when little Hans Goodman, the shy kid at the back of the line, started bawling. Everybody turned back to look at him with assorted sarcastic gapes and sneers.

"Hans, what's the matter?" Calvin asked.

It was incidents like this that could get a camp counselor

in big trouble. Igniting a crying jag from a ten-year-old would invite the camp's business office to make an inquiry into competence and motive.

"I don't want to die!" Hans cried. "I don't want to shoot rifles anymore. I want to go to the library and read."

"You're a stinking little pansy retard," Richie said.

All the kids began chanting "stinking pansy retard," and Hans started wailing and ran away from the group. Calvin chased after him halfway across the soccer field and then grabbed him by the back of his red and black Charlie Brown striped T-shirt while the kids kept chanting, "Pansy retard, pansy retard!"

"Hans, it's all right. You don't have to shoot. And to hell with those assholes—those kids don't know shit. You're better than all of 'em."

Calvin didn't realize he had just sworn until Hans looked at him with wide, reverent eyes like he had found a new best friend. Rather than apologize or correct himself, Calvin merely patted Hans on the back and said, "That's it; *now* you get it. One day you're gonna lead these kids to freedom. You know what the Gospels say, don't you? 'The first shall be last, and the last shall be first.'"

"I'm Jewish," Hans said.

"Oh." Calvin was a little taken aback—they were in a world of WASPs—but thought about it. "What kind of Jewish name is Hans?"

"I'm named after my father, who changed his original name, Hiram, to avoid being imprisoned during the holocaust. He fought for the Polish resistance and kept the name Hans so that we'd never forget."

"Oh," said Calvin. "Well anyway, let's go back and deal with these numbskulls and march to the library." Hans seemed a touch disappointed that Calvin refrained from using swear words again to describe the other campers.

The other kids were now circled around Richie, watching him play with his new miniature Swiss Army knife. One of them saw Hans and called out, "The pansy's coming back!"

The rest of the kids were about to start chanting again, when Calvin yelled, "Shut the hell up, you little creeps!"

All the kids, including Hans, started giggling. Everybody fell back in line and waited for Calvin's orders.

"OK, little numbskulls—forward, march!"

The group started marching, but it quickly turned into a casual walk as they crossed the old estate and headed on toward the academic hall. They fell into complete disarray as they passed the redbrick maintenance house and then the school infirmary. The rain had only modestly moistened the kids' T-shirts, and their hair had a slight dewy quality that reminded Calvin of when he was that age. Back then, there were no pressing urgencies like Susan Vincent or the Vietnam War in his life.

When they got to the library, the kids were greeted by the geeky librarian, Mr. Warner. He was delighted to have some young customers to whom he could teach the wonder of books. Calvin himself had learned to hate books due to Mr. Warner's boring presentations, particularly when he went on about his own masterpiece, *Poo Poo in Paradise*, a novel that told the story of how the Polynesians used their own poop to fertilize breadfruit or something.

"Mr. Warner, we know you're a busy man, and I'm sort of required to take care of the kids by myself anyway, so maybe you can go back to whatever it is you do around here, sir."

"Well, all right then, but I'm available if you need assistance, Calvin. Reading is my specialty." He laughed and walked across the polished wooden floor to his office in the back.

"I don't want to read," said Richie. "I want to shoot guns, like James Bond." The other kids joined in, and Calvin was afraid Hans would start crying again, so after some quick thought, he intervened.

"No, we're not going back to the range today. You have a whole summer to shoot rifles. Today, I'm going to read you a letter from my brother at UCLA."

The kids groaned again, but they all sat down at a long, dark, wood-stained conference table in the middle of the library and reposed in varied postures of boredom.

Calvin reached into his back pocket and pulled out the envelope and slid the handwritten letter out and unfolded it.

He cleared his voice and looked up at the kids to make sure they were paying attention.

Dear Calvin,

It is with great sadness that I report to you from the Western Front that things look more hopeless now than at any time in our lives.

Our brothers are being killed in scores "over there" across the Pacific in that tropical cesspool of violence known to us as the Vietnam War.

Our Vietnamese brothers are not calling it the Vietnam War. To them it's the American Colonial Incursion or something quite similar, I'm sure. It's just like Muhammad Ali said, "No Viet Cong ever called me a 'nigger.'"

Calvin, I can't overstate the severe necessity of your being able to carry the message of liberation back to our brothers and sisters in Lake Forest. We can bring the fascists down from within if we can convince their young ones that class divisions only lead to a sick and fractured world filled with hate and violence. Of course, they themselves are privileged and would never have to taste the blood of war (nor shall you or I due to our own wealth and status), but if Kent State has taught us anything, it is—rich or poor—we are no longer safe in our homes or on our college campuses. Soon they will make it so that only the rich can attend schools of higher learning, and they will control the curriculum so that no one will ever know the meaning of class contradiction and oppression. The fascist life will become the normal one.

I beg of you, Calvin, help me keep this from happening. It's now or never, brother. This is our one and only chance to stop the overthrow of America.

Your brother in Revolution,
David

The children sat around the long conference table tapping their fingers and staring off at the copies of Rembrandt and Matisse that hung on the walls of the main library room.

"Does anyone here know where UCLA is?" Calvin asked.

Tim Cleary raised his hand, and when Calvin called on him, he turned and pointed out the side window and said, "It's stopped raining; can we go back to shooting?"

All the kids yelled, "Yeah!" in unison.

During the short time it took Calvin to read his brother's letter, the rain had stopped and the sun had even begun to peek out from the clouds.

"No," Calvin said, "it's still too slippery, and besides, the rain could start again any time."

"Oh shit," said a voice tucked among campers.

"Who said that?"

Several kids giggled, but no one was confessing. Calvin knew it was futile to find the recalcitrant, and besides, he wanted to discuss the letter while there was still time left in the period.

"If any of you swears again, I'll wash your mouth out with soap!"

Finally, they were silent, and Calvin explained to them where UCLA was and asked, "Can anyone think of how the war in Vietnam might be an example of class struggle in America?" There was no response; the kids were all looking down and around.

"Well then, can anyone explain how racism comes into play in this war?"

Immediately Richie Tobin's hand shot up. Calvin pointed to him, and he responded, "My dad says the army teaches Negroes how to be productive citizens, but they never have any gratitude for all that we've done for them."

"Well . . . that's very interesting, Richie, but—"

Hans Goodman's hand shot up. "My dad says the war in Vietnam is all screwed up, that President Johnson lied to us!"

Calvin felt a breakthrough, but just as he was about to respond, Richie Tobin yelled, "Your dad's full of it! My dad shook President Johnson's hand, and he says that the president is an American hero. He says President Johnson would be a Republican if he weren't from the South. He says LBJ is like Abraham Lincoln, a liberator of the ingrate colored—"

"My dad's not full of it; your dad's just a politician; he doesn't know anything!" Hans yelled.

Before Hans could continue, Richie stood up and started yelling, "Pansy, pansy." The other kids began screaming, and their voices echoed off the high library walls, bringing Mr. Warner out of his office to try to help Calvin quiet the scene.

Out of nowhere a voice shouted above the mad din of the children.

"*Silencium!*"

It was Brigadier General Carlson, the camp director, standing at attention with a whistle around his neck and a polo shirt tucked into his freshly pressed khaki pants.

"What goes on here, children?"

"Sir," Calvin said, "I can explain . . ."

"Calvin, front and center."

Calvin stood up cautiously, as if he himself was being called out of formation to be punished.

"Let's step outside for a moment, son."

The two of them stepped out into the large hallway of the school administration building that used to be a mansion for a Chicago meatpacker prior to the Great Depression.

"Calvin, why are these children not out on the range learning marksmanship?"

"Well, sir, the rain was coming down hard, and I try to practice a certain amount of safety out on the range. Heck, it would be a tragedy if one of our little ones got injured, don't you think?"

General Carlson stood quietly reflecting upon Calvin's words as he seemed to be trying to grasp for words of his own.

"Son, you are aware that there's a war going on, aren't you?"

"Yes, sir."

"We are at *war*, Calvin. This is *wartime,* not reading time."

"Absolutely. I think about that every time I call five campers up to the mat to start shooting."

"Son, I want to make one thing perfectly clear to you. If our American boys can go humping through swamps in Southeast Asia protecting us from Communists, these youngsters can get their shots in here at camp no matter what the weather."

"Yes, sir."

"Now let's go back in the library and sort this argument out."

They walked back into the main room side by side as General Carlson put his arm around Calvin's shoulder in solidarity.

The campers had started acting up again, mostly in ridicule directed toward Hans Goodman, who seemed to be on the verge of tears as he looked up to Calvin for help.

"Silencium," General Carlson called out.

The children were quiet. General Carlson seemed to intuitively read the situation in front of him.

"Richie Tobin and Hans Goodman, front and center!"

The two boys snapped to and then both raced around the table and in front of General Carlson, who was standing at perfect attention.

"What were you two fighting about, anyway?"

"The Vietnam War, General," Richie said. "Hans said the war was—"

"Silencium!"

Richie's face was contorted in resentment as if he was not given the fair hearing he deserved.

"You two youngsters know how we settle things here at Lake Forest Preparatory Day Camp, don't you?"

"Yes, sir," they both said in unison.

"Then it's settled. Ten-hut!"

The rest of the campers scrambled up from the table and stood in a single-file line along the wall. Mr. Warner immediately stepped out and stood at attention in front of the door to his office.

"Left face. Forward, march!"

The children began marching uniformly out of the library and down the long ornate hall of the mansion toward the front entry. Carlson held the door open as they marched out. As soon as they were in formation on the walkway outside the ivy-covered building, he blew a special code on his "silencium whistle," as he called it.

A long blast, two short ones and then a final long one rang out across the wooded estate as a signal to all the campers that they were to drop what they were doing and head directly to the gym. There, a general council was to be held by all the "tribes" and led by the brigadier general.

The campers marched around the corner of the mansion and down the long gravel road they had just traversed, past the infirmary and soccer field, and directly to the entrance of the gymnasium. Carlson blew his whistle in code once more to ensure that all the campers and counselors on the northern end of the campus heard the beck and call.

Children could be seen marching from all four directions led by their teenage counselors, many with clipboards in hand and some with their own smaller whistles around their necks. A counselor had to earn his whistle with a clear record of camper achievement among his tribes.

Hans and Richie's tribe, the Fightin' Iroquois, was the first to enter, and its members went up and sat in their specified spot on the third row of the bleachers. Since the Iroquois weren't Calvin's "home" tribe—his was the mighty Seneca—he found his way to the other side of the entry onto the second row, where he sat quietly until General Carlson waved him over to the back wall of the gym. There he was instructed to grab a thin blue mat, a crate of boxing gear and four safety cones to set along the center circle of the basketball court.

The campers filed into the gym in an orderly manner and began filling the rows of benches that rose up along the south side of the basketball court. When the bleachers were full, General Carlson stepped out into the center of Glory Gymnasium in front of the 120 campers and counselors seated on the bleachers looking down at him. By this time the kids had started gabbing and horsing around, so the general pierced the air with his thunderous voice: "*Silencium!*" he shouted.

He was now accompanied by his sergeant at arms, Godfrey Sparrow, a tall, skinny black kid he had imported from the nearby town of North Chicago, a suburban ghetto community that was near Naval Station Great Lakes. Sergeant Sparrow stood erect as he read through the attendance roster. One by one, each camper shouted "here" as his name was called. After roll call, the general walked over to the center of the mat inside the orange cones and yelled, "Hans Goodman, Richie Tobin, front and center, *now!*" The two boys worked their way off the bleachers and onto the gymnasium floor while General Carlson stood firmly at attention with his jaws clenched. As the boys walked up to him, he grabbed them both at the shoulders and turned them facing him.

"You boys were fighting—it doesn't matter why—and we're going to solve this battle with honor right here in front of the whole camp. Is that clear?"

"Yes, sir," the boys responded softly and in semiunison.

"Each of you, grab a pair of gloves and a leather helmet and stand in a corner of the mat until I blow my whistle."

The boys each grabbed their gear, both careful not to look up at the other. They walked, automatically, to opposite corners of the square as if their spots had been prepicked. They stood looking down as the general blew his whistle.

Hans stepped out from his corner shyly and for the first time looked up into Richie Tobin's eyes. Hans ducked and dodged Richie's fists, but the General walked up alongside him and began egging him on.

"Hans, go to it! I want to see you throw a punch, lad."

Before Hans had a chance, Richie made a direct hit, knocking him back a couple of steps. A roar went up among the crowd. The two boys began swinging madly and ducking each other's punches. Richie was able to connect solidly every four or five swings, and occasionally he would stagger back a few steps for a few moments and then lunge forward. Within two or three minutes (the general didn't seem to be timing the round) Richie landed a straight-ahead blow that knocked Hans to the ground. The campers were all roaring their approval, and General Carlson began a loud count, "One, two, three . . ." However, at "five," it was clear Hans did not want to get up, so General Carlson simply stopped there and grabbed Richie's glove and raised it in the air. The entire camp was screaming its approval.

It was over; Richie had won. Calvin could feel the great efforts of his brother, David, crash down onto the mat next to Hans's limp body. The general walked over to Hans, still lying on the ground, and reached down to help him up. As he was yanked onto his feet, tears trickled down the boy's face. The kids lobbed verbal grenades of derision toward Hans as General Carlson put his two hands on Hans's ears and offered him some words of encouragement. As Hans turned, dejected, to walk back to the bleachers, the general gave him a little pat on the butt.

Hans climbed up onto the bleachers as the kids around him pointed and snickered. Calvin's head fell into his hands. And then he remembered the internship at the Mercantile Bank.

NYMTHS, WOODS & COTTAGES

The house was a wreck, but on account of the woods, I didn't care. It was my wife who convinced me to buy the home up in northern Wisconsin, and because of the threat of divorce (it was a playful threat to combat my laziness), I acquiesced and bought the property north of Lac du Flambeau.

As a child, I was always afraid of the woods. My older brother used to tell me ghost stories about men with hooks who claw your eyes out and eat your dogs. On one of the only occasions that I had a chance to spend time in the woods—during a game of kick the can while at summer camp many, many years ago—I was overwhelmed by strange and ugly animal sounds. There were hoots and caws and scampering footsteps—which I couldn't distinguish from my playmates'. I ended up sitting by the can until everybody got bored and came out of hiding to yell at me for being such a sissy.

But I wasn't a sissy, and the proof of that was six years later when I was at the railroad tracks that ran through some woods outside Kenosha, Wisconsin. I was smoking a joint with my friend Jonathan when we heard a strange melodic voice. Jonathan, who was older than me and thus knew things I didn't, explained that the voice was that of a forest nymph and then described what forest nymphs are and what they do. It turns out they hang out naked in the woods in the evening waiting for young men to come visit them. Nymphs romp freely and share their soft, nubile bodies with the brave boys who venture out to be with them. They have magical powers that prevent mosquitoes and other of nature's vermin from interrupting them during passionate lovemaking.

Well, I doubt you'll believe this—and yes, I know we're way off the subject of the cottage in Lac du Flambeau—but I ventured forth into the dark Wisconsin woods that night and, sure enough, came across a nymph-like teenager sitting in a clearing in front of a little fire that hadn't been visible until I hiked around some thick brush. She was my age, sixteen, with wavy, golden blonde hair and was wearing a baby blue halter top and blue jeans. She seemed to have no fear when she looked up at me. I guess it was my long hair that told her I was cool. I'm sure it also helped that I was still holding what was left of the joint Jonathan handed me when he dared me to follow the sounds of the forest.

"Wanna hit of this?" I asked.

"Yeah, sure," she said as she smiled at me.

The next thing you know, Christy and I were sitting next to each other on a log getting acquainted. I explained to her the whole nymph theory that Jonathan spelled out for me, and she was thoroughly intrigued. She didn't know what a nymph was but naturally assumed she must be one since she was sitting there when I came out looking for her. It turned out the strange melodic voice we had heard at the tracks was hers; she had been singing the Procol Harum tune "A Whiter Shade of Pale," which was her favorite song.

Christy was a runaway. She hated her parents, whom I later found to be horrid scoundrels. She didn't tell me at the time that her dad had molested her, but it was clear from her voice that ugly things had been going on in her home.

I told her how my dad was an OK guy (usually) who owned a bar in Kenosha and occasionally let me drink there if I promised not to smoke pot.

She laughed at the "no pot" promise, but I told her that it was actually serious business because his friends were all rednecks and sometimes he'd embarrass me in front of the whole bar, calling me a worthless, no-good hippy who would have dodged the draft to get out of Vietnam if Nixon hadn't ended the war that spring. "A damn shame he ended it too," Dad said. He once even suggested to the bar customers that they might do well to take me out to the parking lot and kick the hell out of me just to make sure I got the point of what it means to be a real American instead of some long-haired, pot-smoking loser.

Fortunately, the Budweiser delivery guy, whom my dad really liked, had long hair and was a Vietnam veteran. Dad's love for him cut me some slack. The Bud guy was actually my best connection for pot. Good weed was the only reason Jonathan and other older kids were friends with me.

Anyway, I share all this to explain why Christy and I took to each other at once.

While we were sitting there by the fire, we heard Jonathan calling my name.

"Nicky, where the hell are you?" His voice was loud but

softened by the crickets. I *so* didn't want to answer him but knew it would create a huge scene if he thought I was lost, and besides, he was sure to find us anyway.

"Over here," I said finally.

A minute later we could see his image in the reflection of the fire. He had a bewildered look on his face as he saw me sitting on a log with such a cute and sexy girl. He tiptoed up to us like he was looking into a fragile soap bubble of a dream and was afraid it would pop.

"Jonathan," I said, "this is Christina. She and I are going to get married."

Before Jonathan could force sounds from his now-disheveled vocal chords, Christy leaned in and gave me a sloppy kiss on the cheek. I turned my head toward her, and she gave me the first open-mouthed kiss of my life. Everything changed at that moment, and Jonathan could see this crazy story unfolding before him and backed away like life had just dealt him a pair of jokers.

So what on earth does this have to do with the new house in Lac du Flambeau?

Well, because of how we met, Christy and I always considered the Wisconsin woods to be our sacred home. Due to economic considerations that later translated into children, we moved to Milwaukee, gave up smoking pot, and started a functional life. I got a decent union job with Miller Brewing Company—the one good thing my dad did for me—and made enough money for us to retire at fifty-five when our two boys had moved out and found their own forest nymphs. Kenosha was now way too developed, so our only hope was to travel up to the Northwoods of Wisconsin, or what was left of them anyway.

We found a beautiful cottage on the water a quarter mile down the shore from a row of vacation homes that were only occupied part of the year. The house was a proverbial fixer-upper, but neither of us had retired for the purpose of working on houses, so, as I said, it was a wreck, but all around us was water and undeveloped forest preserves.

Sometimes late at night, we hear the sounds of young women singing "Whiter Shade of Pale" from out of the woods, and Christy will join in softly as she sits by the fire. It's a good life.

THE J-CAT

The whole fiasco over the Milwaukee Bucks tickets happened at St. John the Evangelist, and you couldn't find a more awkward place than a church to score basketball tickets anyway. Bad Boy was left with little choice, though, and after all, they were front row seats to see Kareem back in Milwaukee.

Kluszewski, Bad Boy's coworker, said to meet him at the humongous church across from Cathedral Square. Otherwise, he would deliver the tickets to Bad Boy's house, and that would be a disaster. Bad Boy had told his old lady, Marge, that he was working overtime at the brewery that evening. She would never let him go to a basketball game on a Wednesday night. She was like a born-again Jesus freak and considered that kind of nonsense immoral, but overtime—well, that was always moral.

Bad Boy begged Kluszewski to drop the tickets off at Chrostowski's bar off Burnham on Thirty-Seventh Street. It was his favorite hangout. He called it the Polack Farm because it was full of Poles. He never said it to their faces though. They were a little touchy about being called Polacks nowadays. It was the 1970s, and everybody'd gotten so goddamn sensitive.

Kluszewski was one of those rare, pious-type Catholics

(almost like an old lady) who never stepped into a bar on a weeknight. Come to think of it, Bad Boy had never seen him at a bar on weekends either, even though everybody—sinner, saint, Catholic, and Protestant—goes to bars on weekends. In any event, Bad Boy had to meet him inside the big Catholic cathedral. It was weird that Kluszewski would have such a hang-up about going to bars in that they worked together in a brewery, for Christ's sake.

Bad Boy sat down at the pew and waited for what seemed like forever for Kluszewski to finish praying. Kluszewski seemed a little peeved that Bad Boy just sat and stared at him while he rested on bent knees on that leather footrest thing Catholics hunkered down on. What the hell did he expect Bad Boy to do? He sure as shit wasn't going to pray to get tickets to see the Bucks play the Lakers.

Finally, Kluszewski sat up on the pew, reached into his pocket, pulled out the tickets, and handed them to Bad Boy. Bad Boy reached into his pocket and pulled out two crisp fifty-dollar bills, but Kluszewski shook his head.

"Don't worry about it, Bateman," he said.

Bad Boy tried to force them on him, but Kluszewski refused.

"This is a church," Kluszewski whispered loudly. "I'm no Heeb moneychanger," and then he looked around to see if he was disturbing anyone.

Bad Boy hated being the victim of charity, but the comment about Heeb moneychangers made him feel safe. He liked that a Polack would call Jews "Heebs"; it was a throwback to his youth, when things were much clearer.

The church business fucked everything up though. It threw

Bad Boy completely off his game, and his usually organized rit-uals fell into some kind of Catholic disarray—a curse of sorts. Catholics seemed to be at war with fun, so Bad Boy generally tried to steer clear of them—except for the ones who hung out daily at the Polack Farm and other bars. Those ones—even the religious ones—were OK.

The long and short of it was that Bad Boy somehow let the tickets slip out of his hand or his pocket or something because when he got to the Upper 90, where he planned to while away the rest of the afternoon until game time, he reached into all his pockets, and goddamn if the tickets weren't there.

He quickly gulped down his PBR and tore out of the bar and back to the church. It was a short but rough walk—mostly because Bad Boy's heart had been beaten mercilessly by a life-time of salami sticks, Pabst Blue Ribbon, and polish sausage. When he got to the church, he rushed directly to the pew where he had dropped the tickets, panting wildly as he searched up and down. He made a hell of a scene pulling several people out of their peaceful prayers—particularly when he called out, "Oh, Jesus Christ, where the fuck are they?" Finally realizing he was in a church and ought to look pious, he got on his knees in the aisle and looked up to the crucified Jesus and called out, "Son of God, give me my Bucks tickets."

Before Bad Boy could stand up, a priest came from out of the dark shadows of the cathedral and was in his face.

"Is there a problem, my friend?" the priest asked. "I saw you were in here an hour ago with my friend Joey Kluszewski. Wasn't that you?"

"I lost a pair of Bucks tickets here while I was praying. They fell out of my pocket, and they're gone. That's what you get for praying, huh?"

"Well, if I find them, how can I contact you?"

Bad Boy turned and walked out. The last thing he needed was charity from a Catholic priest.

He retraced his steps out of the church doors, onto the street, and all the way back to the Upper 90. Those tickets were gone—vamoose, as the Puerto Ricans liked to say. Jesus had screwed the pooch like he always did. Fuck fun, fuck fun, fuck fun.

Bad Boy was supposed to meet his Jew foreman Bernstein at the Upper 90, and then they'd head off to the game at six thirty. But fuck it all—he couldn't in good conscience spend the evening in a bar down the street from the Milwaukee arena after losing tickets to the game. Bernstein had paid him fifty bucks that afternoon. Bad Boy was planning to pocket the money after Kluszewski said the tickets were gratis. Bad Boy had made a big joke that afternoon about how the tickets cost fifty bucks.

"You get it? Fifty 'bucks' for Bucks?" He laughed and laughed. It could have been ten "bucks" or twenty "bucks"; it was still funny.

"What the fuck's wrong with you, Bateman?"

Bernstein looked at him in the break room like he was a goddamn retard. Now he'd have to tell him that some Mexican gang members shook him down.

After guzzling his PBR, Bad Boy got up from the mahogany bar and left the joint. In a deep state of misery, he tried unsuccessfully to flag a cab and had to suffer an hour's walk back to the Polack Farm, where he had decided to hole up for the evening and watch the game on TV. He had earned a night off with the lie he told Marge, and he sure wasn't gonna waste it with *another* lie about how he was let off overtime early.

The long walk back to the Polack Farm was bleak and gray as he passed rows of bare trees and small houses and duplexes, some made of brown brick, others clothed in shiplap paneling. Burnham Street was dotted with stores and factories and cold, empty fields. There was a margin of hopefulness in the dirty black snow that was melting in the gutters and front lawns as springtime sprung in Milwaukee.

When he finally stepped into Chrostowski's, Bad Boy was met with the sound of dice being slammed on the bar and a couple of Poles looking up and shouting at him.

"Hey, there he is. *Bad* Boy Bateman!"

He didn't remember their names and really couldn't give a shit at that moment.

Bad Boy sat in the corner brooding even though his buddies tried to cajole him over to the middle of the bar to play dice and talk bullshit. He realized that he liked his Polacks—they seemed white enough. I mean they *were* white really—just a little goofy—but over the decades the Poles were slowly getting the rhythm of things in the good ol' US of A. It was that new Polish Pope thing that was pushing them along. The Italians had gotten it too. Back in the day, Bad Boy's dad referred to Italians as colored people, but they must have done something because they didn't look colored anymore, and Antonio at the Breakfast Café made decent French toast.

The world had gotten so weird though. You couldn't make a living without somebody trying to drag you down and blame you for your hard work and patriotism. Every year on Flag Day and the Fourth of July, Bad Boy put his American flag out on the front porch of his house. It was the least he could do. He held fast knowing that Ronald Reagan's day would soon be coming.

Unlike his coworkers, Bad Boy felt guilty that he was in a union. Unions had gone downhill since the days of Jimmy Hoffa. They had become anti-American, but business was business, and Bad Boy was grateful for his job.

What was the difference between Puerto Ricans and Mexicans? That was a tough question. You didn't want to mix them up, though, because the ones at work would yell at you, so he just called them all Hispanic.

Herman Borucki wandered down to Bad Boy's end of the bar and sat down next to him. Bad Boy wanted to be alone and would have told Borucki to shove off, but Herman was a big son of a bitch who was a Golden Gloves boxer in the early sixties when whites and Poles still had a fair edge.

"I thought you scored tickets for the game, you ol' son of a bitch."

"Yeah, but I decided not to go. I really hate the Lakers. I don't even like to be in the same stadium with them."

"So the old lady told you that you couldn't go, huh? But at least you made it out to the bar." Borucki laughed.

"No, not at all. I've stopped taking guff from her. She doesn't tell me what to do anymore. Seriously."

"Whatever. You look down in the dumps, Bad Boy. Something bothering you?"

"It was nothing. I mean, a gang of Mexicans were fucking

with me on the way here, and I told them to fuck off, but you know how that shit gets under your skin."

"Damn Mexicans! Where are they? Let's get a posse and beat the shit out of 'em."

"Jesus, Borucki, this isn't *West Side Story*. Let the fuckers be."

"Hey, I may be in my forties, but I can still bust up punks if they pick on my friends."

"They weren't picking on me. I told them to fuck off and they did."

"I hate when that shit happens. I mean, we've given those bastards everything. Even our jobs at the factory, but are they satisfied? Hell no, they pick on my little buddy Bad Boy every chance they get."

"What the hell are you talking about? I'm *Bad* Boy. Nobody picks on me."

"Yeah, yeah, well come down and slam dice with us, buddy. I could use some of your hard-earned money."

Down the bar, Tommy Smolik saw Bad Boy and Borucki talking and yelled, "Hey, Bad Boy! The Pabst here is tasting a bit tart. Did you pull out your little dick at the brewery and piss in the last batch?" Everybody laughed.

"Fuck off, Smolik!" Bad Boy looked at Borucki and said, "Hey, man, I gotta be alone and think about things."

Borucki got up and called out to the bar, "Hey, Bad Boy's thinking!"

"Holy shit. Run for cover," someone said. Bad Boy didn't know who; they all looked alike to him.

For twenty minutes Bad Boy stewed in his juices as he pounded down a couple of PBRs, when suddenly an astonishing sight issued itself before his eyes—a black kid, standing alone, just two feet to his left.

It wasn't like blacks weren't allowed in the bar; it wasn't the 1960s. A decade earlier, a whole pack of Polacks would have been off their bar stools and dragged the colored fellow out the door and down onto the sidewalk. Nowadays, you had fellow black factory workers in the bar on occasion and maybe even one or two neighborhood brothers who'd stop by now and then. Everybody would pretend to be friends and sometimes even say nice things to one another. But for some *kid* all alone out of *nowhere* to walk into the bar was too odd for Bad Boy to wrap his head around.

The kid was wearing a pullover polo shirt and a pair of creased gray khakis. He wasn't dressed 'white' exactly, but he sure didn't sport the kind of outfit that would best accentuate his blackness.

The black kid looked at Bad Boy and smiled. Bad Boy wanted to snarl at him—let him know it wasn't cool to just wander into a neighborhood bar while Bad Boy was stewing and then pretend he belonged there.

The bartender came over and smiled at the young brother almost like he was happy the kid was there or something.

"What can I do you for, young man?"

"I'm looking for Jonathan Bateman. His wife said he might be here."

The bartender pointed to Bad Boy, who now snarled at the black kid involuntarily.

"What the fuck? Are you the pizza delivery boy?"

"Be nice, Bad Boy," the bartender said.

The black kid laughed liked he'd been through this charade a hundred times before. The entire bar was silent, and Bad Boy was sure the kid was going to get his ass kicked if he wasn't especially graceful. But the black kid seemed oblivious to Bad Boy's concerns. He sighed serenely and put his hand into his pocket. Bad Boy was worried he might pull out a gun.

"I found these at St. John the Evangelist; I believe they're yours."

Bad Boy just stared at the tickets and then up at the black kid. Everything Bad Boy knew about blacks made the whole situation seem so totally unlikely. I mean, even Bad Boy wouldn't return front row seats to a Bucks/Lakers game no matter *where* he found them.

"I guess you expect a reward, huh?"

Bad Boy wasn't gonna fork out a penny to this boy. Let him *keep* the fucking tickets. Let him go and swap 'em for a bag of heroin or whatever the dumbass shot up.

"Not at all. I just knew these things shouldn't go to waste, and I asked the priest if he knew anything about them. He took me to the rectory office and gave me the phone number of a guy named Joey, who gave me your home phone number. I spoke to your wife and told her I found your tickets to tonight's game. She said she thought you were at work but if you weren't, you must be at Chrostowski's here."

"You told my fucking *wife* you had my Milwaukee Bucks tickets?"

"Fuck you, Bateman," a Pole called out. They were all listening intently. "Buy the kid a drink. He just brought you a pair of fifty-dollar tickets for Christ sakes." A couple of the other Poles chimed in, "Yeah, buy the kid a drink!"

"Oh no, fellows," the kid said modestly. "I don't drink. Booze doesn't sit well with me. I mean, I used to drink; heck, I used to do a lot of crazy stuff. I'm black and all that." He laughed like maybe he was being sarcastic.

The Poles started howling like they had just made a new best friend. Finally, Borucki called out, "You'll drink a soda, won't you? Come on down here. I like you, kid!"

"I really shouldn't be hanging in a bar on a weeknight. I'm in school."

"Oh come on, guy. Just one," someone called out.

The black kid laid the tickets down in front of Bad Bay and walked down the bar and sat next to Borucki, and then he and the Poles started talking.

Apparently the kid was going to Marquette University. He wanted to be a dentist and was studying premed there before going off to graduate school in Stockton, California, or somewhere. He mentioned something about his hero, a jazz trumpeter named Miles Davis. The kid tried to learn trumpet when he was in junior high school but couldn't play for shit, but he found out Miles Davis's father was a dentist. He figured this was the best homage he could pay to Miles, and damn if he didn't start liking teeth after a while.

This was all very unsettling shit for Bad Boy to hear on Wednesday night when there was a Bucks/Lakers game at the Milwaukee arena. Finally, Bad Boy grabbed the tickets and walked them over to the black kid, who everybody was now calling Dennis—Dennis the Dentist.

"Take these things. I don't want them. I don't take charity."

Dennis looked at him with perplexed contortion in his face. Finally he said, "It's not charity if they're yours."

"Yeah, but now that you found them, it's charity to give them back."

Dennis smiled. "You're a bit of a j-cat aren't you?"

A Pole at the bar, Ex-Con Eddie, recognized the phrase and laughed loudly.

"A what?" Bad Boy asked.

"A j-cat." Dennis seemed to look for the proper words, like he was about to lay a profound definition upon Bad Boy. "A j-cat," he continued "is prison lingo for someone who's uh . . ." he thought carefully like he didn't want to cause offense and then said, "*touched*." He paused for a second. "Touched, yes! Touched by God that is. You're touched by God."

Eddie started howling and slapping his hand on the bar.

"Yeah, yeah," Smolik yelled. "That's it, Bad Boy. You're a j-cat."

The word "j-cat" echoed up and down the bar.

"I'm *Bad* Boy!"

"OK, OK. Don't get so touchy," Dennis said. "People are so sensitive nowadays about what you call 'em."

Bad Boy was about to force the tickets on the black kid when a voice at the entrance of the bar shouted, "Bateman! You *asshole*!"

Bad Boy turned around and there in the doorway with tan corduroys and black rubber snow boots was his Jew foreman, Bernstein.

"Oh, hey there, Allan. I, uh, was just heading over to the Upper 90 to meet you." He held up the tickets to show him everything was legit.

Bernstein looked at the clock. "The game starts in twenty-five minutes, and we got to park and walk to the gate."

Bad Boy was quiet for a moment.

"Hey, Bernstein," he said. "I don't feel so hot. Why don't you take *both* tickets. Hell, the second one's on me. You can find someone."

Borucki pointed at the kid. "Take Dennis the dentist, man. He found the damn things at the church."

Bad Boy looked at Dennis, who was now smiling innocently.

"What's going on here anyway?" Bernstein said. "You *lost* our tickets?"

"Yeah, yeah. I was in church and got all confused in the reverie. Hey, Borucki's right. Take the kid; he's earned it." For some stupid reason Bad Boy patted Dennis on the back and quietly mumbled, "Thank you, kid. I hope you become a great dentist some day."

"Well, let's go, fella," Bernstein said. "It's the Lakers; Kareem's back in town, man!"

Dennis shook Bad Boy's hand. "It was a pleasure to meet you," he said, and he dashed out of Chrostowski's with Bernstein, who put his arm around the kid's shoulders.

"So, what's your name again, son?" he asked as they walked out the door.

MAYPOLE MADNESS
A Fairy Tale—The Final Chapter

They burned their own flag. Crazy and sick, the children screamed like witnesses at the Salem witch trials.

"We're done with you," they shouted on a gray morning in Appleton. "We're done with your money and your complacent ignorance."

They had guns and knives. Twelve-year-old Tommy Talbot was their leader. "A sociopath" was what the doctors said. "A sicko" was what all his classmates said—until—everything came to the brink.

Tommy led the children into their own homes while their parents were off at work. One by one, they broke into their daddies' arsenals, grabbing weapons that the families proudly owned in the name of "freedom."

Tommy had already raided his father's gun trunk in the basement. He hacked the padlock off with a metal cutter that hung above the tool table. How stupid, he thought, to padlock a trunk and then leave a tool to open it twenty feet away.

He also thought Father was stupid to molest his own son and then leave him alive to even the score. But Father always assumed he was mentally crippled—too damaged to ever harm anyone.

Father didn't know that Tommy was a different person when he was away from home. Tommy's teachers would constantly warn the old man that the boy was a "ticking time bomb," but that only made Father laugh. Sometimes when he was touching Tommy, he'd say, "Are you a ticking time bomb, boy? No, I didn't think so."

On this epic morning, the timer was set to go off.

The school principal and his staff were frantically on the phone trying to contact parents.

"Where are your children?" they asked. "How come no one's at school today?"

It was the great Day of Reckoning. Jesus said it would come—children rising up against their parents—a new order was set to begin. Far and wide, across the nation, angry kids would remember what happened in the town of Appleton. They too would rise up in insane defiance; nothing of the old regime would be left standing.

Before a shot was fired, they tossed Molotov cocktails through the windows of their parents' homes. Tommy taught the children how to make them as, one by one, the suburban homes burned in Satanic richness.

"The insurance companies will pay out, and the banks will refinance," he yelled over the roar of the first burning house. "But then we'll torch 'em again, and we'll keep on doing it till the banks and insurance companies go broke!" The children roared their approval as they danced from burning home to burning home in maypole madness.

"They want a toxic environment?" Tommy screamed. "We'll give 'em a toxic environment. Suburbs ablaze across the nation!

They'll have to kill us all, kill their own children—Johnny and Jimmy and Suzy and Kay." He raised his fist in angry defiance. "If they want their sick little world back, it'll be over our dead young bodies."

At high noon, the children arrived in the Appleton town square like little minuteman militia. From first grade to eighth, they carried holstered guns on their sides and rifles up to their shoulders.

Tommy had a handheld rocket launcher from Father's arsenal. "Let the first shot be echoed around the world," he said and then fired a rocket through the window of the local bank.

The children shouted hurrahs in prepubescent mania as the rocket exploded and fire and shrapnel burst out through the doors and windows of the bank.

People poured out onto the street screaming "terrorists" until they saw their sons and daughters across the street with rifles and bayonets pointed toward them.

The roar of sirens could be heard in the distance, and then five police cars screeched in front of the town square, and officers piled out with their bodies squatted low, protected by their car doors. And then, around the corner came an armored SWAT wagon with a machine gun turret on top.

The mayor appeared on the sidewalk with a megaphone.

"What is it that you want?"

"We want nothing!" Tommy screamed. "You have nothing to give us but this fucked-up world filled with war and exploitation and lies. Children lie in poverty across the globe while your filthy-rich, swine leaders speak treatises on how everything must be this way on the road to prosperity.

"They say, 'We'll share our wealth with you as soon as you give us just a little bit more and work just a little bit harder.' Like greedy, dope-pushing junkies, they promise us the world just as soon as we give 'em the shirts off our backs.

"And we're done with economic collapse and global debt and shithole schools and *A*-rab scapegoats. The war on terror is a war on us! And the Mexicans—let's blame it all on the Mexicans—poor migrants who just want a plate of food for their children."

The town's Presbyterian minister grabbed the megaphone and appealed to Tommy. "Tommy, it's me, Reverend Arnold. You can talk to me."

But Tommy had tried to talk to him to no avail. Tommy had visited him several times.

"Father touches me," he would say.

The minister had told Tommy to buck up.

"You'll never get anywhere with talk like that."

Parents lined the sidewalks behind the principal, calling out to their children across the street, "Please, please, stop this madness. Come home. You're too young to understand."

The children picked up rocks off the ground and started throwing them at their moms and dads. A police captain grabbed the principal's megaphone and yelled, "You kids need to disperse now, or we will begin firing."

The parents screamed, "No! No! It's our children! Johnny and Jimmy and Suzy and Kay."

At Tommy's mark, the children pulled the rifles off their shoulders and aimed them at the police cars. The police captain with the megaphone shouted, "This is your last warning."

An officer in an armored vest appeared from the roof of the SWAT wagon, placing himself behind the shield of the machine gun turret.

Tommy yelled, "Fire!" and the young militia let go their first shots at the police.

The megaphone man, yelled, "Fire!" and the policeman in the turret and the other officers hidden behind their open car doors began shooting.

The policemen shot, and then they shot some more, and then they shot some more while the parents on the sidewalk screamed. After a minute and a half of firing, a hundred children lay dead in a pile in the town square.

Never before in the nation had there been a slaughter like this. At the memorial, blood tears were cried. Tommy Talbot was held the culprit.

"Nobody, and I mean nobody—none of the children—would ever—could ever—think up such a horrific thing on their own," said the Reverend Arnold, who presided at the event in the still-bloodstained town square. Tommy's father stepped up to the pulpit and apologized to the town for having a sick and rotten child.

As the proceeding was going on, militias of children were arming themselves across the nation. Soon they would be out on the streets ready to die for Tommy Talbot's cause. If moms and dads throughout the country wanted a sick, unjust world, that sick world would die with their children. There would be no new generation to carry it on.

THE PLAID GOLF PANTS

Apparently, when the police first arrived, the standoff was already intense. Mr. Duffy, the dry cleaner, was out in the backyard yelling up at the second-story window.

A half hour earlier, he had been dropping off shirts and pants to Mrs. Rosewood's preferred delivery spot, just inside the garage, when little Margaret snuck out to his truck. She grabbed a pile of clothing and ran inside the house, locking the door behind her. Duffy figured it was simply a juvenile prank and ran to the back door and started pressing on the doorbell incessantly. He continued until he heard pounding on the second-story window and discovered Mrs. Rosewood holding the clothes and waving down at him. Assuming that she would now run downstairs and deliver the clothing back to him, he sighed.

"Oh, thank God," he said.

To his surprise, Mrs. Rosewood held up a can of lighter fluid and a barbecue torch, threatening to burn all the items (including a plush mink stole) unless Mr. Duffy returned a pair of her husband's golf pants that he claimed he never received. She mimed the words *"I want the golf pants"* in a clear and exaggerated manner so he would know exactly what she was talking about.

Duffy reported all this to Inspector Roland McDermott, who was dispatched to the scene because he was the town's lone hostage negotiator and this was the closest they had ever come to a hostage situation.

McDermott's captain thought he would be delighted to finally get some work in his trained field, but Roland was less than thrilled.

"I didn't sign up for shit like this," he told the captain as he grabbed his jacket and walked out the door of the police station.

When Roland arrived, two uniformed officers were standing on the back gravel driveway with Styrofoam coffee cups in their hands. Steam was rising from the cups as one of them took a sip after nodding at McDermott. Mr. Duffy was still standing, looking up to the second floor window where Mrs. Rosewood had her arms folded around the clothes as she smiled down on him in smug confidence. Duffy looked back at the two cops and pleaded.

"Do something! This is my business she's messing with!"

"Are you insured, Mr. Duffy?" one of the cops asked.

"Well, yeah, but this kind of thing's still bad for business."

The officer pointed at Roland, who was approaching them, and said, "Well, McDermott here is a hostage negotiator. If he can't bring her down, then we're gonna have to storm the place and take her by force. Quite frankly, I doubt she's gonna set the clothes on fire because it would probably burn her house down."

McDermott stepped up to one of the cops, the taller of

the two.

"So who reported this thing?" he asked. He then pointed at Duffy like he was answering his own question.

The cop shook his head. "The next-door neighbors did, but we've ordered them to stay inside. They heard the screaming and apparently thought Duffy here was a rapist trying to get at the occupant."

"That's a damn lie!" Duffy said. "Her little girl stole my clothes. You've got to do something about this."

"Calm down, sir," Roland said. "What's the woman upset about, anyway?"

"She bought some stupid golf pants," Duffy said. "They were apparently for her husband's birthday. She claims she needed to get them fitted properly; he's one of those weird sizes between full and obese. I never saw the goddamn things—I swear—but she says she dropped them off at my shop. The lady's bonkers, officer."

"*Detective*," said McDermott.

"OK, *detective*. Now get those clothes back before she ruins them."

"Tell me exactly what happened here."

Duffy proceeded to explain the business about the girl sneaking into his vehicle and grabbing the stack of clothes.

"Where's the daughter in all of this?" Roland asked.

"Fuck if I know. She's probably tied up downstairs until the crazy bat needs her for her next psychotic mission."

"Mr. Duffy, an attitude like this doesn't help the situation at all."

"I'm not the one holding a stack of clothes hostage, detective."

"Does she have a phone number I can call?"

Duffy pulled his cell phone from his pocket and began scrolling through his customer contact list until he found her name and handed the phone to McDermott. Roland held Duffy's phone up in front of his face with his left hand while he began punching out the numbers on his own phone with the thumb of his right. He then handed Duffy's phone back to him.

The number rang a couple of times as he looked up at Mrs. Rosewood. He could see her lay the clothing down in front of her against the windowsill, reach into her pants pocket sheepishly, and pull out her phone.

"Hello," she said.

"Hello, Mrs. Rosewood?"

"Yes, that's me."

"Hi, I'm Detective McDermott."

"Oh, hi! How are you?"

"I'm fine, thanks, Mrs. Rosewood. How are you?"

"I'm fine."

"Mrs. Rosewood, it seems we have a bit of a disagreement here."

"Yes."

"Would you be willing to come down here and talk with us?"

"No."

"You'll be perfectly safe. I promise. We are, after all, the police department."

"I know what's going on, detective. Mr. Duffy has you all in his back pocket."

"Actually, ma'am, I've never met Mr. Duffy before. I don't

think anybody here has."

"It doesn't matter. People like him have connections to city hall. If I turn over these clothes, he'll just deny his guilt and skate by, and I'll lose Ronnie's new golf pants. I paid good money for them at Macy's."

While Roland was talking, Duffy seemed to awaken and called out to the cops.

"She dropped the clothes! You've got a clear shot. Shoot her!"

Roland turned to Duffy and shouted, "Shut the fuck up!"

As he was yelling, Mrs. Rosewood grabbed the clothes with her right hand and pulled them in front of her while she cradled the cell phone between her ear and shoulder. She picked up the lighter fluid and began to lift the spout with her left thumb in a slow, deliberate manner.

"No. Please, Mrs. Rosewood, you don't want to do that. Let's see if we can find a way out of this."

"I'm not gonna be target practice for those kill-happy cops!"

"Nobody's shooting at anybody, ma'am. Mr. Duffy lost his head. We're mature and trained policemen. We don't take orders from an agitated bystander."

"*Bystander?*" Duffy said. "My livelihood's at stake. She might as well be squirting that lighter fluid on me. This is a form of assassination. Hell, it's *character* assassination."

McDermott looked over at the two uniformed officers. "Could one of you get this man out of here?"

"I'm being held hostage! You can't do this!"

One of the cops stepped over to him and put his left hand on Duffy's upper arm and started tugging. Duffy tried to shake him off.

"You don't want to get into it with us, sir," the cop said. "Believe me. It'll go badly for you."

Duffy grumbled but acquiesced to the policeman's grasp and was escorted down the driveway to a squad car, which was parked at the curb. Meanwhile, the sound of fire truck sirens could be heard ringing through the neighborhood. In the distance, Roland could see neighbors approaching Mrs. Rosewood's property. He turned to the other officer.

"Rusty, I need you to do crowd control; I'll take it from here."

The cop sighed. "Anything you say, detective."

McDermott looked back up at Mrs. Rosewood.

"It's all settled, ma'am. It's just you and me. Let's talk about this like friends, OK?"

"I don't know you."

"Well, this is a good time to get acquainted. But first, I need to know your daughter's safe."

"She's safe unless Duffy gets his grubby hands on her."

"Well, can I see her?"

"She's not here."

"Where is she?"

"She's on an errand."

"You swear she's not in the house with you?"

"Yes, I swear. Why would I lie?"

"No reason. So tell me, do you like golf, Mrs. Rosewood?"

"My husband likes golf. Anything that's good for Ronnie is good for me."

"I bet he's a nice man."

"He's a wonderful man. A good husband. A good father."

"How would he feel if he was here right now witnessing

this, Mrs. Rosewood?"

"He wouldn't understand, but that's beside the point."

"Is it, Mrs. Rosewood?"

"Yes. He's a modest man who could never admit his own worth. But I know it; and Margaret knows it too. That's why we have to do this."

"Is Margaret your daughter?"

"Yes. Look, there's no way to prove Duffy took the pants, but I remember placing them in the pile with a note and little markings on the waist and cuffs. I've never trusted the man anyway, but he's the only tailor in town."

"They must be mighty fine pants then, huh?"

Mrs. Rosewood put the lighter fluid down and grabbed the phone from out of the crook in her neck.

"Oh, you've never seen anything like them—Scottish plaid on a soft cotton fabric. They're the only ones I've ever seen like that. And the only ones on the rack."

"You like plaid, do you?"

"Yes. Ronnie and I went to Scotland on our honeymoon. It was the only cruise we could afford that September."

"Sounds like a memorable trip."

"We spent our first night in a real-life castle near Edinburgh. Oh, and you know, in Scotland they don't pronounce the 'burgh'; they say '*burrow*.' Anyway, the next morning we were awakened to the sound of bagpipes. It was the most exotic experience."

"Wow, that sounds very nice, Mrs. Rosewood. And I didn't know that thing about the 'burrow.'"

Roland could hear the roar of a fire truck as it rolled up out front. He looked down the driveway as one of the cops, the taller one, Henry, waved the truck to a stop and a couple of firemen jumped off the side. He watched the fire chief screech up in a red Crown Victoria.

"What's all the fuss?" Mrs. Rosewood asked.

"Oh, it's the fire department. We have to call them just in case. We wouldn't want you to catch fire or burn down your nice home."

"Oh no, it's OK. I've got this all figured out. I have a pale of water here by my foot to throw on the clothes as soon as they're ruined."

"You know water can spread lighter fluid and make the fire expand out of control."

Roland didn't know why he said that. He guessed maybe it would make her realize she'd gone a little overboard and surrender.

"You're making that up," she said.

"I wish."

"Well, I've committed myself to this. If I back out now, I'll look like a fool."

"Mrs. Rosewood, in all sincerity, if you set your house on fire, you stand a much better chance of looking like a fool. Believe me, I'm a hostage negotiator, and I'm not supposed to be talking like this, but we're friends now, aren't we? I can tell you the truth."

"If we were friends, then you'd believe me about the golf pants."

"Mrs. Rosewood, the cost of a burnt-down house has got to be more than a stolen pair of trousers, don't you think?"

"The house won't burn down, detective. I've got control of

the situation."

"Maybe, maybe not. And what about all those clothes? Should you put other people's property at risk because of the behavior of one man?"

"He's got insurance. He can reimburse them."

"Mrs. Rosewood, I beg of you to please come down here, and let's talk this thing out face-to-face."

"Not on your life! Your marksmen will have to shoot me out of here. Then we'll see how Duffy feels. That son of a bitch will probably relish in my death. There'll be nobody around to make him feel guilty about his new pants. He can wear them freely out on the golf course whenever he pleases."

As she was finishing her sentence, the shorter cop, Rusty, walked halfway up the driveway and got McDermott's attention. He pointed to his watch and mouthed "time's up!"

"Oh, for God sakes," McDermott said.

"What?" Mrs. Rosewood said.

"Not you, ma'am. I was talking to one of the officers."

Roland looked over Rusty's shoulders and saw three additional police officers wearing flak jackets; one had a crowbar.

He shook his head forcefully, but Rusty ignored him and turned back to the three SWAT team members and pointed to the front door.

McDermott turned and looked up at Mrs. Rosewood. "They say I can't negotiate with you anymore. You've got to come down."

"They'll have to drag me out through the fire, detective. I'm sorry. In this story, the underdog wins." She shut off her phone and put it in her pocket.

McDermott waved to get her back, but she ignored him and picked up the clothing and the lighter fluid.

Roland turned to Rusty, "Get in there fast!"

Rusty gave the order, and McDermott could hear the front door being cracked open. He ran down the driveway and around to the front door. He followed the men as they raced up the stairs just across from the entryway. Mrs. Rosewood was standing at the top of the staircase on a landing in front of the window. She had just set the torch to the clothing, and a little flame burst up from the pile on the floor. One of the officers pulled her away as the other one looked into the bucket. He picked it up to pour onto the fire, but Mrs. Rosewood screamed. "No, no! It'll spread the lighter fluid."

The officer stopped just before the first drops of water sprinkled out. "What the hell is in this?"

"Water," she yelled.

He shook his head and proceeded to pour it on the clothes, and the flame quickly sizzled out as McDermott reached the top of the stairs. Three firemen in full gear, one with an axe and two with extinguishers, came charging up the stairs behind him and began foaming the burnt pile of clothes. The hallway smelled of steamy smoke, and there was a black carbon stain on the ceiling above Mrs. Rosewood, who stood with a police officer holding her.

"We need to check the house out just to make sure everything's OK," a fireman said.

"Do what you have to," said Roland. He turned to Mrs. Rosewood. "Ma'am, we need to take you downtown. I hope you understand."

"Yes, I understand. And it was worth it."

The officer who had been holding her back started to reach for his handcuffs, but McDermott stopped him.

"That won't be necessary, will it, Mrs. Rosewood?"

"Oh my, no."

She and the group of policemen proceeded down the stairs and out the front door. As they were stepping outside, Roland heard a cry from the front sidewalk by the street. "Mommy, Mommy, I found them!"

Little Margaret was running to the door with a pair of plaid golf pants. Suddenly, Duffy broke away from the policeman who was holding him by the squad car.

"Why, you little brat! Give those back to me."

He started chasing after her as she ran up to the door and pulled herself behind Detective McDermott. Duffy tried to reach for her, but Roland grabbed him, and then one of the uniformed officers pulled Duffy back while reaching for his baton.

"Mommy, they were in his office," Margaret said, pointing at Duffy. "One of the workers there took me right in and pulled them out from under a stack of newspapers. He had them hidden away."

"*Who* took you into my office?" Duffy said.

"I don't know, but she said she was from Asia."

"Leta—that whore. I'll deport her so fast!"

"What about the pants," Mrs. Rosewater said. "What were you doing with my pants?"

"Those are *my* pants, goddamn it. I paid for 'em!"

"Then how come they were hidden under a bunch of

newspapers?" Margaret asked.

"It's none of your bratty little business where I keep my clothing."

Mrs. Rosewood lunged toward Duffy and had to be restrained by one of the officers.

"Look," Roland said. "We can work this stuff out at the station. Rusty, handcuff Mr. Duffy here."

"Handcuff *me*? I was the goddamn hostage. On what charge are you dragging me down to the station?"

"Sir, you're disrupting a police investigation."

Mrs. Rosewood smiled. "I knew it would all work out! Oh, detective, you *are* a friend after all. Let me introduce you to my daughter, Margaret."

"Hello, Margaret."

"Hello, sir," Margaret said. "You're my hero! Will you come over for a barbecue when my dad gets back?"

"That sounds very nice, dear. Let's talk about it down at the station. We've got some business to take care of."

"That sounds fun!"

"It's a lot of fun. It's what I live for."

VENUS & MARS

"Now that's balls," she said. She pointed up to the wall across from the bar at an autographed poster of Harrison Ford from *Raiders of the Lost Ark.*

Norman looked at it with indifference. "He's just a freaking actor, Cassandra."

Cassandra had a curious way of handling arguments. There was an alternate-reality sense to the manner in which she debated those points that were dear to her heart. Norman, on the other hand, was intensely logical and practical and believed he had a pretty decent bead on things.

It was an odd relationship anyway. Unlike every girlfriend Norman had had in the past, Cassandra was trying to push him into a life of adventure and grave risk. Typically, the theme of his past relationships—at least as they approached long-term and possibly marriage—was that it was time to settle down, make some money, and worry about the future. Norman himself had happily acquiesced to that concept on his own.

Cassandra was from a rich and privileged family though. Or at least she said she was, and the two brand-new Jaguars that her parents bought her over a three-year period seemed to validate her thesis.

"The whole point of art," she said, "is to imitate life and create inspiration. I think Indiana Jones is the ideal role model for you, Norman."

"I'm not sure what you're driving at, Cassandra. Do you want me to quit my insurance job and travel the world looking for lost treasures?"

"I don't know. I think you would be happy if you really got out and did something in life—made an impact."

"I'm happy right now. Hell, I'm happy here at the Rusty Hammerhead having a martini with you."

Cassandra smiled. Norman was satisfied that one of his best skills in life was to deflate Cassandra's aggressive control issues with a simple compliment or word of affection. It was easy for him. She was a pretty lady whose long, reddish-brown hair screamed dirty things at him. If photos of her were in a fashion magazine beside top-line models, he'd choose her in a split second even though she didn't quite have a model's body or accentuated features.

Cassandra picked up her martini, which was full, with an untouched olive resting on the bottom, and put it to her lips.

"You're eyeballing my olive," she said.

"Sorry, it's just a habit that goes back to when I was a kid."

"Really?"

"My dad use to drink a martini before dinner, and I always tried to coax his olive from him. I love the taste of a gin-drenched olive."

Cassandra laughed. "Well, eat your own fucking olive, Norman."

"Oh, I will. I'm just waiting for it to juice up."

"So what, you want to eat *my* olive in the meantime?"

"Not at all. I'm just looking at it." He then lifted his eyes up to her cute round breasts. "There's something else I'd rather be munching on."

"Control yourself, little boy."

She sighed and looked over at the brass, nautical-looking clock above the cash register at the bar. "Speaking of eating, what's taking so long for our seats? I thought I saw empty tables in the restaurant."

"People probably called in and reserved them."

"On a Wednesday night?"

"We can find another place if you want."

"No, I just feel like the bar here is a bit of a sleazy bringdown."

Norman looked around. The crowd was dressed semiupscale—men in khakis and button-down shirts and women in expensive designer jeans. It seemed mostly to be office workers from the Embarcadero Center having happy hour cocktails before heading home into the San Francisco fog.

"It doesn't look particularly sleazy to me. It's just designed this way to resemble a turn-of-the-last-century longshoreman's saloon."

"Whatever. I expect an entourage of nineteenth-century whores to descend on this place any second."

"Whores? They'd be wasting their time. Most of the men have women with them—hot babes like you. Well . . . nobody's hot like you."

"You *are* frisky tonight, Norman."

Norman smiled at her and lifted his martini and drank a big gulp. It was strong—almost straight gin—and took him by surprise, making him cough.

Cassandra laughed. "Too much of a man's drink for you, huh?"

She grabbed her drink and took a big deliberate gulp from it and then grabbed her olive by the toothpick and put it between her teeth as she stared at Norman suggestively.

"If you want this olive, you have to earn it." She tried to speak seductively through the olive, but it came out garbled, making Norman laugh. He grabbed his martini and took a big slug to demonstrate that the previous gulp was just a minor glitch to his manliness. Cassandra let her teeth sink into her olive and then sucked it into her mouth and munched on it in mock reverie. Norman pulled his olive out and did the same. After a moment they both burst out laughing.

A woman's voice from the entrance to the dining room called out "Becker, party of two."

"*Finally*," Cassandra said.

The two of them stood up together and grabbed their martini glasses from the table. Norman caught the eye of the hostess and raised his glass to signal they were coming. She ignored the gesture and turned and walked back into the dining room.

"She's not very cheerful," Norman said.

"What, is she supposed to jump up and down and say 'Oh, it's you!'? She's got a restaurant full of customers, Norman."

"A maître d' is supposed to be a greeter."

"She just greeted you, dear. Get over it; let's eat."

As soon as they were seated at their table and the waiter stepped up, Norman ordered a bottle of chardonnay. Cassandra deferred wine choices to him because he always made her happy.

His choice of white wine for the evening was strategic in that the restaurant was located next to Fisherman's Wharf, and

Norman felt that seafood would be the most appropriate entrée for dinner. The Rusty Hammerhead wasn't necessarily a seafood restaurant, but he stood by his principles. He felt safe that Cassandra would follow suit because, though it was a bit archaic, he had instructed her that she must always have white meat with a white wine.

"Chardonnay?" Cassandra said. "I guess we're having chicken for dinner."

"Seafood, dear."

"Why? They've got a lot of great stuff here."

"We're next to the Wharf. It's only polite to support the locals in the area."

"What the hell are you talking about?"

"Whatever. Get what you want. The sea bass is great though."

They were silent for several moments as they settled into their seats.

"So I've been thinking," Cassandra said.

"Really?"

"I've been thinking you ought to consider signing up for one of those programs where they train people for a Mars exploration."

"What? What the hell are you talking about?"

Once in a while Cassandra would completely zing an idea from left field. It was quite odd—though kind of cute.

"They've started programs where candidates train for a trip to Mars. You know, spend six to twelve months in a hostile terrain in space suits and live in a cramped cubicle like they would on Mars."

"Is this your way of breaking up with me?"

"No, what do you mean?"

"Six to twelve months in isolation? That's insane. We'd never see each other again."

"I researched it. They allow conjugal visits every eight to ten weeks since it's only training."

"Who does? What on earth are you reading on the internet?"

"It's the whole Mars settlement thing. There's a NASA program as well as several private groups that are working on it."

"You want me to go to Mars?"

"Maybe. But in the meantime you could provide a great service to humanity by testing the lengths of human endurance in isolation."

"So, what would you do while I was locked up in a capsule for six months?"

"I'd think about you all the time and send you little messages to make your heart go pitter-patter and hope you would do the same. I wonder if they let girlfriends send dirty videos to the astronauts while they're en route to Mars."

"Actually, Cassandra, I think their plan is probably to send couples up in space so that issues like sex don't sidetrack the astronauts and drive them insane."

"Would you go insane without sex for six months?"

"Hell, I don't want to find out."

"What if I sent you naughty videos of me?"

"I'd rather you just send them to me now."

Cassandra giggled as the waiter walked up to the table with the bottle of chardonnay and an ice bucket. He handed the bottle to Norman, who examined the label carefully and then handed it back. The waiter uncorked it with a delicious pop that made Cassandra noticeably shutter. He picked up

Norman's wine glass and gave him a generous pour. Norman tasted it and nodded his head at the waiter, who then grabbed Cassandra's glass and gave her a big pour as well.

As he walked away, Norman held up his glass and said, "Here's to Mars, my love." They clinked their glasses.

"Really?" Cassandra said. "Are you going to do it?"

"Hell no! That's insane."

Cassandra put her glass down and sat silently, her face blushed with embarrassment. Suddenly she started crying.

"Oh come on, baby," Norman said. "I didn't mean *you* were insane. I just think there are better ways to express our love than me isolating myself for six to twelve months."

"I just want you to be happy!"

"I am happy. For Christ's sake, I love being with you."

"But it's deeper than that. I want to be your muse. I want to be the Oona to your Charlie Chaplin, the Eleanor to your Franklin."

"How about just the Cassandra to my Norman?"

"I'm already that."

"The point is," Norman said, "whatever I do, I want to do it with you, baby. If I'm going to be an international archaeologist or an astronaut, I need to have you there with me."

"But it's so dangerous! Would you really put *my* life in jeopardy just to have me with you?" Her tone got harsh, and her eyes squinted with umbrage. This was the irrational, angry side of her that Norman hated. Still, principles were principles, and he had to be firm.

"Your life?" he said. "What about mine?"

"Yes, exactly. It's always about you, isn't it?"

"No. I mean, you want to send me off on a death-defying trek just to vicariously fulfill your fantasies."

"It's not vicarious! I'd be home rooting for you the whole time. And besides, you're a man. You're required to take the risks in life."

The waiter came back to the table but saw that they were talking and had not picked up their menus.

"I'll give you two lovebirds some time," he said.

"We just sat down," Cassandra said.

"Thank you," Norman said. "We'll be ready in just a few moments."

The waiter smiled weakly and spun toward a table in the next row over.

"So," Norman said, "do you want to try the sea bass?"

"They don't have oceans on Mars."

"Oh, Jesus. Will you stop it, Cassandra? This is some kind of insane obsession all of a sudden. I'm not going to Mars."

"I didn't say you had to go to Mars—just train for it. They pay you well, and we could have the type of affair couples dream about."

"Dear, the affair couples dream about is a cruise to Bora Bora or the Greek Isles—not a year of separation with occasional conjugal visits."

"I can't talk to you if you're not going to be rational."

"So what do you say? Sea bass?" Norman grabbed his martini glass and drained the rest of it with one heavy swig and put it toward the center of the table away from the full wine glass. Cassandra took her martini glass and did the same.

"Do you notice how much our mannerisms are the same?"

she said.

"I guess."

"You guess? Norman we're kindred spirits sent here on a mission."

"Where? The Rusty Hammerhead?"

"Stop it, Norman. You know what I mean."

"Not exactly, but please go on."

Cassandra folded her arms and glared at him. Norman knew the look. She was going to silently scorn him through the meal and into the rest of the night—possibly through the next day—if he didn't loosen up and sincerely pretend she wasn't batshit loony.

"I *am* serious, Cassandra. Proceed. And remember, I'm just an insurance man. I need your guidance to see the deeper shades of life."

"Oh, for God's sake. Don't mock me."

"I'm not. I'm being serious."

"OK then. Ever since we first met four years ago at AT&T Park—alone in adjacent boxes—and both screamed, 'Get 'em Panda' in unison when Sandoval stepped up to the plate, I knew we were cut from the same wood."

"That *was* kind of weird; I had just noticed you sitting there moments before. But hell, it's been a few years; Panda left us— went to Boston to get fat and then return as a fucking traitor."

"What—he did his job. He brought us together. His career's mostly done anyway."

"True. And he got the last out for Bumgarner to win us that World Series."

"Oh, the memories. But Norman, it's been like that ever

since we met. We both shout expletives together at exciting moments like a couple sharing Tourette syndrome."

"Yes, I've noticed that, darling, but I've just gotta ask, what does that have to do with going to Mars or even an archaeology dig deep in the Congo?"

"*An archaeology dig in the Congo.* That's beautiful, Norman!"

"Anyway, please proceed."

"OK, so, between the two of us, I'm the dreamer—the visionary—and you're the technocrat. Destiny has thrown us together to leave an indelible mark on the world. Whether it's to find the lost Ark of the Covenant or lead mankind out into the Milky Way galaxy, we have a mission, and if we thwart it, we will surely die."

"That's pretty scary. How about if you dream up a nice house for the two of us, and I arrange to have the thing financed and built."

"You don't have any money, Norman. You're just an insurance man. I'd have to dream it up, finance it, and have it built all myself."

Cassandra had a good point. That thought was rather depressing for Norman. In reality, he didn't have much of anything going for him—or with her for that matter—other than her. But what if she was right? Serendipity had clearly pulled them together. Maybe she and her money were God's gift to him for practicing discipline and adhering to a simple life.

"You know," Norman said. "T.S. Eliot was an insurance agent—or was it a bank teller? I can't remember."

"Why are you telling me this?"

"I don't know. I was just thinking aloud."

"You can always go back to insurance after you make your mark. I'm sure T.S. Eliot was quite happy counting cash after he won the Nobel Prize."

The waiter came back over to their table. "Have you decided on anything?"

"No," Cassandra said. "We just *got* here!"

"How about an order of oysters Rockefeller," Norman said.

"See?" she said. "That's what I'm talking about, Norman! You know how to navigate and I know how to dream."

"I'll have your order right up while you two look at the menu," the waiter said.

"Sea bass," Norman said after the waiter walked away.

"Sea bass, what?" Cassandra said.

"That's what we're having for dinner. That's my navigation, my destination for the evening."

"Oh, we're getting so close to Mars; I can see the glare of the red rocks up ahead."

"It will surely match your beautiful red hair."

"See! You'll be thinking of me the whole time!"

"So, do you like the wine?" Norman knew she hadn't tried it yet, so this would buy him some time to change the subject somehow.

Cassandra picked up her glass and took a slug. She closed her eyes as she drank it in, and a smile appeared on her face.

"I hope they have wine on the rocket ship—at least for big occasions. It seems only fair for all the work you'll be doing."

"Dear, it's cramped space and very crowded. I think they only pack condensed food up there anyway. I don't think they even bring bottles of Tang anymore."

"Can you imagine how much you'll be pining for me and a glass of dry chardonnay if you do this? When you come home, we'll have a night to remember for the eons."

"So, you didn't say; how was the wine?"

"It's delicious. It's always delicious, Norman."

"Look. I don't want to wreck the night, but we're going to have to find something a little more realistic than pseudo space exploration."

"You're really frightened by the risk, aren't you?"

"It's not the risk that worries me; it's the loneliness. I simply have to have more time around you to survive. Now, *that* risk, the risk of insanity by separation, would be too much for either of us."

"That's so romantic, Norman."

"Maybe I can fight wildfires in the Sierras."

"Oh get real. You'd be burned alive in a second."

"A policeman?"

"You can't handle a gun without flinching, and you're a lousy fighter."

"I could get in shape. Take boxing lessons."

"Be realistic, Norman. You're weak and uncoordinated; your attribute is your brains. That's why you're in insurance."

Norman looked over at the waiter, who was leaving another table, and got his attention. When he came to the table, Norman asked for two orders of sea bass.

"Would you like it served after the oysters Rockefeller?"

"Of course we would," Cassandra said.

"That would be great," said Norman. "And we'll both have mashed potatoes to go with it." The waiter scribbled down the order and was about to walk away when Norman had a thought.

"Hey, do you have a girlfriend?"

"I'm gay."

"He means," Cassandra said, "do you have a lover—a significant other that you care about."

"Yes, I do."

"Well," Norman continued, "how would you feel if he were to sign up for a trip to Mars for a year?"

"I think it takes two years—eight months each way and another six months or so on the surface until the planets realign for a straight shot back."

"Don't be difficult," Cassandra said. "He just wants to know how you'd feel."

"I support my boyfriend in everything he wants. But I would probably want to go with him."

"What if you couldn't?" Cassandra asked.

"Then I'd wait for him."

"Would you think it romantic?"

"I'm not sure what you mean."

"I mean, would you wait patiently back home, maybe compose emails and videos?"

"You mean like dirty videos?" The waiter suddenly seemed aroused.

"Exactly! Yes!" Cassandra said. "Oh, admit it. You'd love it."

"Well, I'm not sure that would be my first preference, but yeah, I guess that would be romantic. Hell, as soon as Carlos got back, our first night together would be one for the eons."

"Yes, yes! Thank you! Now go get those oysters. You know they're an aphrodisiac."

"Oh God, yes. I know that." The waiter laughed. "They're my favorite too! I just knew you two were wild little lovebirds the moment you sat down."

"Now go and do your job. Norman and I have business to discuss."

The waiter turned and wandered off to another table.

"So, I think it's settled then," Cassandra said.

"What's settled, Cassandra? Hell, you led the witness. All his answers would be thrown out of any court."

"How did I lead him? I asked him straight questions, and he gave me straight answers."

"But you phrased it out of context."

"You're doing it again."

"Doing what again?"

"You're being irrational."

Norman sat silently for several moments, staring at his wine glass. Suddenly it felt as though he had truly been cornered. It was as if she had checkmated him. Was he really going to Mars or at least a colony in some desert? He tried to wrap his head around this totally mad moment and find a way out. The waiter appeared from behind him with the oysters Rockefeller. He moved Norman's wine and martini glasses and placed it in front of him on the table.

"I must say," the waiter said. "I truly admire your courage. I would be proud to call you my boyfriend. Make this night one to remember." He poured a splash more wine into each glass and then grabbed the empty martini glasses and walked away.

"A night to remember," Cassandra said.

Norman lifted his wine glass, and they toasted like newlyweds.

"A night to remember."

THE GURGLING COUP

There were too many to count—it was a disgrace. Mrs. Goldberg baited them into Baker's Park, where all they did was stumble around squawking, farting, and ruining Davenport's peaceful weekday mornings.

Davenport had retired early in life because he was a smart investor. He had planned his life decades ahead, living frugally through the years. When he left home for college, his dad taught him, "A smart man thinks about the golden hay when the grass first starts turning green." His dad was chock-full of wisdom like that, and Davenport had waited half his life to sit on a park bench and dispense those chestnuts to the local high school kids.

Just like back in his own day, high school kids wandered into Baker's Park during their class breaks to study and hang out and sometimes even smoke cigarettes. Davenport himself had to quit smoking some fifteen years earlier due to a doctor's ultimatum, but his dad had told him, "A few sins now and then are a strong man's virtue."

Davenport lived alone in a modest, rented apartment across from Baker's Park. He had plenty of dough and could have owned a house somewhere, but his dad taught him, "Property is for buying and selling, not loafing upon." He liked his simple life save for Mrs. Goldberg downstairs. She often looked at him askance in the hallway and seemed to be against everything he stood for. In the past it had only been a mild annoyance since they both worked every day and communicated rarely.

The problem now was that Mrs. Goldberg, a mothball-infested crone who kept her hair up like a silver knitting ball, had decided to retire from her mindless librarian job at the exact same time that Davenport left his investment business. So, low and behold, Baker's Park was going to be her new home too.

Every day she brought a plastic garbage bag filled with bread slices that she picked up in an alley behind an Italian restaurant in town. At the end of the night, the proprietor made sure to leave her a healthy stash beside the dumpster, and she would swing by at eight in the morning to collect it on her way to the park to feed the pigeons.

Everybody loved Mrs. Goldberg. But everybody didn't have to live above her in an apartment building or now be forced to sit across from her in the park. To Davenport, the woman was a sad-sack witch who promoted filth and pestilence in public places. So on this early April morning, Davenport decided it was time to take some action and end the Goldberg charade for good.

Davenport's former job was in and around the stock market, which had given him ample opportunity to learn how to deal with enemies. There were many angles of attack, but for the weak and feeble such as Mrs. Goldberg, the best method was to destroy the opponents' support structure and leave them alone and exposed, naked and sick.

Unfortunately, he couldn't very well go around town spreading nasty rumors about the old bag. Actually, he could, but it would be risky. She was a "sweet" little old lady with a spotless reputation, and Davenport was an aggressive broker with a—well, let's just say there are a lot of ugly stereotypes about his kind of people.

No, his character attrition would have to be subtler. Plus, he had his own reputation to build among the high school students to whom he would dispense Father's precious lessons once Mrs. Goldberg was disposed of.

He watched her from across the square while sitting on a worn wooden bench. She sat on the other side of a concrete fountain where a fat, little angel spit up dirty, reclaimed water into a big round basin. Davenport sat motionless as he stared down the Goldberg lady, who busily tore apart bread slices and tossed them at eager little rat birds. They gurgled before her in an ugly, ecstatic choir and walked in stupid circles like a moron looking for his car keys in the grass.

Davenport finally stood up, walked around the fountain and across the square and stood before the old woman. The pigeons scattered timidly and stubbornly as he approached. Mrs. Goldberg was mildly irritated by the commotion but put on a good-neighbor smile. She looked up at him with eyes of wisdom—the wisdom one gains from sitting in a building full of books for forty-five years.

"Why, hello there Mr. Davenport. So nice to see you in the park on this beautiful, beautiful spring day."

Davenport looked around and saw only sickness.

"It's not spring. The trees are still dead. Not much beauty in a park full of dead trees and dirty pigeons."

"My, somebody woke up on a lumpy couch this morning, didn't they?"

"I slept fine. The only lumpy thing I see is a park stuffed with grimy little winged rodents."

"Now, now, you stop that, Mr. Davenport. These little friends have never done anything to harm you. They have as much right to God's earth as you do."

"This isn't God's earth. It's a people's park. And they don't belong to God's earth anyway. They're little mutants that would die in a second if batty old broads like you would just let nature run its course."

"Stop it this instant, Mr. Davenport!"

"My father used to say, 'Nature that can't fend for itself is Darwin's greatest bane.' These pigeons are proof of the death of God."

"What's gotten into you? Why aren't you working—plundering the poor? Are you drunk, Mr. Davenport?"

"No, Mrs. Goldberg, I'm not drunk. I'm here as an officer of humanity to ask you to obey local ordinances and stop feeding these sick animals. This is against the law."

Mrs. Goldberg turned livid and slammed a newspaper she had been holding onto the bench next to her.

"There is no law. There are no signs posted. If you don't cease and desist in this abuse, I'll show you the real law."

A couple walking their dog were approaching just into earshot, and Mrs. Goldberg looked over at them and back at Davenport, almost daring him to continue his rant.

"There is a way out of this, Mrs. Goldberg."

"I don't want a way out of this. I want to be left alone to feed these poor birds."

"Not for you, I mean. For me."

"What. Leave? Go back to your barbaric high-rise downtown? Go and manipulate the markets while millions of Americans watch their dreams melt into burning, rusted trashcans where they warm their hands during the cold, ruthless nights?"

Pigeons scattered as the couple approached with their dog. The couple glanced at Mrs. Goldberg and then at Davenport. They seemed ready to jump in and assist her when suddenly their Great Dane jerked them forward as it chased a lone pigeon that hadn't scattered fast enough. Davenport watched as the dog was about to pounce on the frightened bird, but the pigeon quickly took flight, barely escaping the dog's paw and landing on a tree branch safely above the park. He looked at Mrs. Goldberg and smiled. Evidence was on display even as they spoke—pigeons were doomed in a world without Mrs. Goldbergs.

"You can spew your literary spin all you want," Davenport said. "I'll tell you how I plan to solve this. Have you ever seen what Alka-Seltzer does to a bird?"

"What??"

"Alka-Seltzer, my dear Mrs. Goldberg, gets inside a pigeon's gut and causes all the food to expand like a balloon full of helium until the bird explodes into a confetti blast of feathers and intestines. It's really a grotesque sight, if you want to know the truth."

"Are you threatening to blow up the pigeons? I'll call the SPCA immediately. They have jails for sick people like you."

She looked over at the couple in a plea for support, but they were too busy wrestling their agitated dog to pay any attention.

"No, I'm not the one who'll blow up the pigeons," Davenport said. "You will!"

"What kind of sick, twisted, lack of logic are you trying to lay on me, you brute?"

"I'm going to poison all your bread. I'm going to spike it with Alka-Seltzer."

"You're mad!"

"Only just mad enough to deal with you."

"I don't believe you. That would take hours of your time and cost a fortune in Alka-Seltzer."

"I may not have a lot in my life, Mrs. Goldberg, but I do have time, and I do have money."

Mrs. Goldberg stood up from the bench and tied up the plastic bag filled with bread slices. She looked down at the flock of pigeons, many of which had found their way back to her feet.

"Come, my little love children, let's get away from this man. He's a lunatic. A *lunatic,* I tell you." She looked at Davenport straight in the eyes, pointing her finger. "You'll never get away with this. As God is my witness, you'll spend the rest of your days in the booby hatch."

"You'll see," he shouted as she walked away. "Those fat infestations will literally be farting their guts out. This whole square will be a sea of blood and pigeon intestines." He felt a demonic possession overtake him and started to laugh as Mrs. Goldberg moved quickly to a bench at the far corner of the square with her birds in full tow. She glanced back at him in darted anger and then down at her precious flock.

Davenport turned to walk back to his bench when he beheld a high school couple walking directly toward him. They were young and beautiful and full of life. He felt like a magnet pulling youth toward his wisdom.

"Hey, kids," he called out as they approached. They began to veer to the left to get past him. "Hey kids, let's sit down on the bench. I've got something to tell you."

The girl pulled her arm tightly around her boyfriend's waist as he snarled, "Not interested."

"No, no. You don't understand. I want to tell you about love."

"Not interested," the boy repeated as they walked past Davenport toward the other end of the park, presumably to the Burger King across the street.

"Listen," he called out as they walked away. "You're new to this love thing. My father told me, 'The first bright fire of youth is a blinding one.' You need to understand this. It's like a parable."

They scurried away quickly. The girl gave a furtive glance back as she held the boy tightly.

That was all right—there were plenty more like them. His father once told him, "Many see the trough on the horizon, but only the mighty attend the feeding." Or was it "the drinking"? He couldn't remember and wished he had taken notes, but he hated his father back then, and it was enough that he was able to remember the words of wisdom.

He turned behind him to see Mrs. Goldberg attending to the growing flock of birds at her bench. She looked serene in a sickening sort of way, and it made him loathe her more. If only he had known Mrs. Goldberg in his youth. He would have hated her and could then have had room to love his father.

It was clear by her calm demeanor that she didn't really believe that he had it in him to poison pigeons. Davenport's plan had simply been to try to scare her into seeking police protection for the birds, and then perhaps she'd try to convince the storeowner to hire a watchman to guard the day-old bread through the night. She was just the kind of stupid broad who would insist on something like that and immediately transform herself from a sweet old lady to a needy old hag that people would run away from.

But now Davenport felt he had been dared. "No man is a man who turns down a dare, no matter how stupid it be," his father taught him. How utterly true this was as he stood now at the precipice of his retirement years.

It was a forty-minute drive each way to the Rite Aid pharmacy in the adjacent county. Davenport realized that if someone really wanted to make an investigation, it would be easy to discover that he bought out a store full of Alka-Seltzer even if it was out of the immediate area, but he was satisfied that nobody could possibly take a bunch of dead pigeons that seriously, let alone do an autopsy.

The bright lights on the pharmacy floor and the countless security cameras made Davenport nervous. He found his way to the indigestion aisle and grabbed every box of Alka-Seltzer and its generic equivalent off the shelf. Looking at the sixteen boxes in his handbasket, he realized it was not enough to do the trick, so he dropped all but one of them on the aisle floor and wandered back to the pharmacist's area, stepped up to the window, and called out to a man with white hair and glasses wearing a lab coat.

"Sir, I need a couple of crates of this stuff," he held up the Alka-Seltzer box and waved it at the man's face.

The pharmacist stood staring at him with a phlegmatic expression.

"May I ask what you're planning to use that substance for?"

"What. Is it illegal all of a sudden to buy Alka-Seltzer?"

"It depends what you're planning to make with it." He pointed up to a wall behind the cash register where there were boxes of ephedrine-related products like Sudafed and such and a sign reading, "By law we can only sell two boxes per customer."

"What are you implying?"

"I'm not implying anything, sir. I'm asking you what your intentions are with the Alka-Seltzer."

"So, you're saying a grubby old lady can feed pigeons in a public park, but a middle-aged man heading into early retirement gets cross-examined for buying an indigestion remedy?"

"Pigeons? Old ladies? Have you been smoking meth, sir?"

"What kind of pharmacist are you? You can't make meth from Alka-Seltzer! It's goddamn aspirin and fizzy shit."

"Sir, I have to ask you to watch your language."

"If you want to know the truth, I'm buying this stuff for my son's middle school science project. He's doing a demonstration on geysers in Yellowstone Park."

The pharmacist took a deep sigh and laughed.

"Oh, well, why didn't you say so?" He picked up the phone

and paged a store clerk, who phoned him back immediately.

"Billy, go to the storeroom and find me a crate of Alka-Seltzer—"

"Two crates," Davenport said.

"Two crates, Billy." And he hung up.

He smiled and shook his head. "You really had me fooled with that line about old ladies and pigeons."

"I wasn't trying to fool anyone, mister."

"I understand. It's just that pigeons and old ladies are a sweet spot for me. My aunt Zelda just retired from her library job, and she's dedicated the remainder of her life to feeding the birds in a park across the street from her apartment."

Davenport stood still as the pharmacist gave him a deep and serene stare, smiling at the graceful memories of his relative. Davenport recognized that sick, serene gaze. He looked down at the pharmacist's name badge. It read "Sydney Goldberg."

"Yes, well, that's a delightful memory," Davenport said. "Old ladies are sure cute, aren't they?"

"Oh, Zelda is the sweetest thing."

"I love pigeons."

Billy the stock boy approached the window with two crates of Alka-Seltzer as Sydney Goldberg rang up the order. Davenport put it on his Visa card. As he turned around, a uniformed police officer stepped up to the red line in front of the pharmacy counter.

"May I ask what you're planning to do with all that Alka-Seltzer, sir?" he asked.

"Aw, it's nothing, Tommy," the pharmacist said. "It's for his kid's science project. Hell, you and me did the same thing back when we were in school, remember?"

"Actually, dad bought us flares," said the cop, "and we almost burned the classroom down. Remember that?" The two of them laughed as Davenport stood nervously.

"By the way, officer," Davenport said. "You can't make meth from Alka-Seltzer. It's just aspirin and fizzy stuff."

"Hey. I'm just *asking* is all. Do you want trouble?"

"No, sir."

"Anyway, Tom," Sydney said, "I've got your prescription ready back here in the bin."

"That's good; it's a half-hour drive to work . . ."

Davenport turned around and carried the two cardboard crates out of the store to the parking lot, where he loaded them into the back seat of his car.

It was eleven o'clock at night when Davenport, wearing a black trench coat, stepped out of his car at the curb adjacent to the alley behind Tarentella's restaurant. He opened the rear passenger side door and pulled out the two crates of Alka-Seltzer. He kicked the door closed with his left foot as he proceeded to carry the crates to the back of the alley, where he espied a black plastic garbage bag sitting in the reflection of an incandescent street light. He laid the crates on the ground by the bag and sat down next to them. He ripped open the top of one and pulled out his first box of Alka-Seltzer. He opened it and put it on his lap and then untied the black garbage bag filled with day-old bread.

Just as he was peeling open the first aluminum packet with

two tablets inside, a pigeon flew down from the sky and landed on the crate. Davenport flinched, and the tablets flew from his hand. One landed on the crate beside the bird's talon.

"What the hell are *you* doing here, you little nocturnal mutant?"

The bird ignored him and stuck its head down and broke the Alka-Seltzer tablet up with its beak. As Davenport sat frozen, the pigeon carefully gobbled up the entire pill and then jumped up on top of a dumpster and looked down at him while making that gurgling coo that Davenport found so objectionable.

Davenport stared back with equal fascination. This was the moment of truth. In a matter of minutes, the pigeon would be an explosion of guts, feathers, and carcass dripping from the metal trash bin. Davenport looked at his watch while he tried to remember how long it took a tab of Alka-Seltzer to fizz up in his glass and then how much longer before he would feel relief in his stomach.

Meanwhile, the fat, feathered animal just perched there and stared him down. It was a battle of nerves, but the little fellow didn't know that the cards were now stacked against him.

After a number of minutes, nothing happened, so Davenport reached over on the pavement where the other tab had landed. He tossed it up to the bird, who leapt slightly and caught it in its beak and then laid it down on the lid of the dumpster and began breaking it up like the first one and then ingested it in a couple of quick jerks. It looked back at him again.

Another long time passed, and nothing happened. Finally, the bird flew up in the sky and alit upon the gutter of the restaurant roof making other sick but innocuous noises obviously designed to annoy Davenport.

All of a sudden a car pulled up, blocking the alleyway, and a spotlight flashed on Davenport sitting on the pavement. The light blinded him, but he heard a car door open and the sound of a two-way radio blaring in the background.

The voice of a police officer called out, "I got a drunk here in Bronson's Alley. I could probably use some backup."

"Copy that," the radio said, and then "08, what's your twenty?" and so forth.

Davenport could now see the shadow of the officer as he strode around the front of the car holding a long flashlight in his hand like a weapon. Davenport started to get up when the cop stopped him.

"Sir. I'm going to have to ask you to sit still and put your hands where I can see them!" Davenport held out his hands above his head as the cop approached him. The cop turned on his flashlight, which was unnecessary in the blare of the car's spotlight, and shined it on the open box of Alka-Seltzer. He then let the flashlight beam roll over to the open bag of bread on the other side of Davenport. He started laughing.

"Alka-Seltzer and French bread? That's a new one. What kind of sick perversion are you into?"

"No, sir." Davenport scrambled for an explanation. When his mouth opened, words spewed out randomly. "You see I get an upset stomach when I eat bread and . . ."

The cop laughed harder. "What the hell are you talking about? Have you been smoking meth? When my partners get here, we're gonna give you a few exercises to test your sobriety. In the meantime I need for you to slowly pull out an ID and hand it to me."

Directly above the policeman, the pigeon started cooing. The cop looked up and stared at it for a moment and back down at Davenport and then at the Alka-Seltzer and the bread. A light bulb seemed to go off in his mind.

"Holy shit! You're trying to poison the pigeons, you sick fuck."

"What are you talking about?"

"Don't lie to me. All my life I've heard of bastards like you. Going out to the seaside and trying to kill flocks of seagulls."

"It doesn't work. Really. I mean look at the pigeon. He's just fine."

The cop looked up at the pigeon, which looked down at him briefly and then over at Davenport.

"Man, if I could arrest you for attempted homicide right now, I would." He raised the back end of his flashlight. "I carry this thing for scumbags like you!"

Davenport heard the sound of a second squad car pulling up and saw the flash of red-and-blue lights. He heard another radio blaring and car doors opening.

Two new cops appeared at the entrance to the alley.

"What we got here?" one of them called. "Another drunken pervo whacking off in the alley?"

"Even worse," said the officer standing with Davenport. He pointed to the box of Alka-Seltzer and the bag of bread. "He was trying to poison the pigeons."

"Holy shit, what kind of evil . . . Wait a minute!" He shined a flashlight on a faded sign on the redbrick wall that read Tarantella's. "This is where my Aunt Zelda picks up her day-old bread." The cop pulled his flashlight off his belt and started to lunge toward Davenport, but the third cop held him back.

"It's not worth it, Tom. You'll get suspended, and this bastard will be back out on the street killing pigeons with his crummy lawyer suing us."

"*Get up!*" Tom said. "Get your ass up now and put your hands on your head." He looked at Davenport in the light and then at the crate of Alka-Seltzer. "You son of a bitch! I remember you! I *knew* you were a slimy felon. Get up right now!"

Davenport, with his hands in the air, did as instructed, and the first cop asked him to turn around. As he turned, Tom grabbed both his arms in a radical jerk and ripped them down behind him. Davenport screamed in pain, and then Tom put handcuffs on him and shoved him face-first into the brick wall of the restaurant.

"Man, this bum isn't worth taxpayers' money in a damn jail cell," Tom said. "We should just take him out to the woods and bury him."

"It didn't work," Davenport said with his face smashed against the bricks. Blood trickled down the wall from his nostrils. "The joke was on me. Please! Look at the pigeon. He's fine."

Tom pulled Davenport back as he and the other three men all looked up at the pigeon, which leaped off the gutter into the air, hovering above them. All of a sudden it started making another gurgling sound, but not through its mouth—this time it was from inside its body. The bird's fluttering became irregular as it started to vibrate. The four men in the alley all braced themselves for the moment of horror. The pigeon fluttered directly over Davenport, made a throat-rattling squawk, and then promptly spewed bird shit all over his head and jacket. Immediately it flew up and off into the night sky.

The cops laughed hysterically. They slapped one another with high fives, and finally the original cop turned to the other two.

"You know, there's not a whole lot we can book this shit-head for, except maybe vagrancy, and that's a helluva lot of paperwork for very little."

"Damn," Tom said. "You're probably right." He looked at Davenport and then put his hand on his holstered gun. "If I ever see you a hundred yards from a pigeon, I'll kill you."

"Yes, sir." Davenport said. He looked down at the Alka-Seltzer crate and then back at the cop. "My father once said, 'A man once warned, who twice missteps, deserves three times the penalty.'"

"Yeah. I'd say that about sums it up," Tom said. "You need help. I think you ought to check yourself into the booby hatch."

He turned Davenport back around facing the wall and removed his handcuffs. Tom fastened the cuffs back onto his belt as the three officers walked back to their cars. Davenport watched hazily as the cops walked away.

"You know," he heard the third cop say, "that Alka-Seltzer thing's supposed to be an old wives' tale."

"I don't know," said the first cop. "There was this delinquent in junior high school who swore he did it with some seagulls while he was on vacation in Santa Monica . . ."

The conversation faded into oblivion as the cops disappeared into their squad cars and off into the night while Davenport stood alone in the alley. He pulled a handkerchief out of his raincoat pocket and began to wipe the bird droppings off his head as the cops drove off.

CHRISTA'S CASE
A View from the Borderline

Eat a peach. That's all Stephen could think of as he looked out his dormitory window at Christa in her short cutoff jeans and flowery pink blouse with the front tied up in a knot, exposing her beautiful peach belly. Sometimes looking at her aureate smile and curly blond hair was too much. She had a desperate look in her sixteen-year-old eyes, the look of a reckless waif about to lay waste to her life.

It was nearing the end of summer—the Midwestern dog days—and the twelve "chosen" students, holed up in the old Montgomery Hall dormitory, were gearing up for three weeks off before the fall semester of 1973. The Allman Brothers Band was blaring on the stereo—a long and melodic jam from *Eat a Peach*, which sprayed day-glow colors across Stephen's room like a mouthful of psilocybin mushrooms. The chosen students— all frowned upon as losers and freaks by their classmates and professors—took great pride in their capacity to understand the arts and sciences in a manner unintelligible to their fellows. To Stephen, arts and sciences were typified by the Jefferson Starship album *Blows Against the Empire*, the story about a band of renegades who hijack a starship and take it to freedom.

The summer session was an eight-week program that brought slower students up to speed before the start of the coming semester. Historically, students with Stephen's academic record would have long before been expelled from Montgomery Academy, but in 1973, the prep school was trying a new strategy of taking recalcitrant students with high aptitude and working with them privately to see if they could be reformed. This was mostly because the area's best and wealthiest teenagers were no longer interested in attending Montgomery; their families shipped them back East to Exeter and Andover and other prestigious New England establishments.

Stephen had no desire nor felt any need to be reformed. In truth, he merely wished to be left alone to imagine a life with his beloved Christa. In his fantasies, they would hitchhike together cross-country and settle down in Seattle. He had once seen a bunch of runaway kids in Seattle during a layover when his parents took him to Spokane to meet unknown relatives. He was sure Christa and he could hook up and find a new life in that city.

Christa had run away from home in June and landed at Montgomery Hall to crash with an old junior high school friend, Tyler, now a senior, whom Stephen worshipped. Tyler played electric bass and had long black hair in a ponytail.

It was odd that even though Stephen and his cronies were considered delinquents, the only "supervision" they received was from an old alcoholic math teacher named Mr. Potter. He as much as told them that so long as they left him alone to do his thing, he would leave them to do theirs. This was the 1970s; it was like that. Some parents even let their kids drink beer and smoke pot in the basement as long as they didn't try to steal the car and go joyriding. Sex was prevalent too although Stephen had yet to get laid. Margaret Pearlman once stuck her hand down his pants, and he reciprocated, but that was as far as they had ever gotten, and they were drunk at the time. Stephen wasn't interested in Margaret otherwise, and she didn't appear to be interested in him. They smiled gamely at each other in the hallway between periods.

Talking to Christa took great courage. It was confusing because she treated him so kindly; it should have been easy. Once on a Friday night they all camped out by the railroad tracks with a keg of beer and a bag of weed. Sprawled out in his sleeping bag, Stephen lay next to Tyler and Christa, pretending to fall asleep with a lit cigarette in his hand. He did this to get her attention—and it worked. She leaned in and shook him gently.

"Stephen, you'll burn yourself, baby."

She called him "baby"—it was the sweetest moment of his life.

Christa's relationship with Tyler puzzled him. It appeared that she slept on the floor of his dorm room in a sleeping bag. Stephen found this hard to fathom. He'd go nuts having her in his room unrequited. Thinking about it gave him a chill up his spine.

Stephen got up from the old wooden desk in his room and walked out the door and down the hall to the dorm's back entrance to catch Christa, who was hanging in the parking lot. It was all he could do to simply step outside into her world uninvited, and he felt like he was risking everything just crossing that line.

Jethro Tull's *Benefit* replaced the Allman Brothers as it blared out a dorm window upstairs.

"And if she feels like dancing, no one will know it . . ."

As he walked out the back door and around the corner, Christa saw him and burst into a big smile. Her smile radiated the warmth of a thousand suns, but surely it couldn't be intended for him; he knew that. She was leaning back against Tyler's jeep but jumped forward and approached him, offering him her open arms. He had no choice but to embrace her; it was joyful and disturbing at the same time.

"Hey, Stephen."

"Where's Tyler?" he asked.

"His father came by and picked him up. They're going out to lunch."

"What are you up to today?" It was Saturday, but Stephen knew that didn't make any difference to Christa, and in fact, the question was rhetorical.

"I was thinking about going out to the railroad tracks and smoking some weed or something."

"That's cool. I got some if you want."

"Yeah, that would be real cool."

Stephen felt intense queasiness in his gut and tightness in his chest. It was like he had just asked her on a date. The last time he felt that anxious was the previous autumn at an All-Prep Cross Country Invitational in Wisconsin. He competed against forty-five other boys on a 2.5-mile course at St. John's Military Academy, where he ended up finishing tenth. It was his fastest run ever—fourteen minutes, seventeen seconds—

and he hoped that those same intense pangs he was feeling were an augury of good fortune with his beloved.

"I gotta go back to my room and grab my pipe and stash," he said.

Christa held up her blue-green crocheted purse and said, "I got mine right here; you can go get yours later."

He was overjoyed that there might be a "later" with Christa.

The trail through the woods to the railroad tracks carried the aroma of dried summer beauty. The morning dew had hours ago evaporated, and it was gearing up to be another scorching suburban day.

"Hey," Christa said. "Maybe after we get stoned we can go swimming in that pond across the pasture."

"Sure."

Stephen wondered if they would be swimming in their underwear—or would they strip down entirely? The embarrassment of getting a hard-on suddenly plagued him.

They sat on an iron rail next to each other on the tracks and passed the pipe. After a couple of tokes, the gravel bed beneath the railroad tracks took on the subtle texture of fluorescent pink and green patterns. The patterns always appeared when Stephen smoked pot—ever since his first acid trip two years prior. Dimensions would become distorted, and the world seemed to jet out from his consciousness as if he were Jimi Hendrix's guitar.

After passing the bowl a few times, they heard the soft blast of a horn in the distance and looked south down the tracks. A tiny, single white headlight was shining out on the horizon. After a couple more tokes, the headlight grew larger, so they stood up and retreated to an old brick wall that surrounded the campus. They pulled themselves up onto the sturdy bough of a tree that had fallen on its side many years before. Next to them were the ruins of an old gatehouse. It once served as the private train station for the estate of the Chicago meatpacker Bartholomew Holcombe that had graced the site of Montgomery Academy. Holcombe threw himself in front of a speeding locomotive from that very spot during the crash of '29.

The area around the gatehouse was cooled by the shade of several old oak and pine trees. In a flash the train poured by. Stephen expected a freight train with forty or fifty cars, but it was the Olympian Hiawatha headed north to Minnesota and then across the west to Seattle. He recognized the train from its dome and Milwaukee Road sleeper cars. Stephen wished he and Christa were on that train, maybe with their own private compartment.

After the train rolled by, Christa looked at him demurely and, struggling to sound confident, said, "Let's do it, guy."

The two of them crossed over the tracks to the path that led to Bannockburn's cow pasture. Stephen had spent much of his teenage life there drinking and smoking and hanging out. It was where he first comprehended his favorite two words: "pastoral" and "bucolic." He invented his own phrase once when he was high: "pastoral bucalia."

They trudged across the grasslands, avoiding cow pies, and stumbled into stoned giggles as Christa grabbed his shirt to keep her balance.

When they got to the pond, they smiled at each other shyly.

"Do you suppose the water's OK to swim in?" Christa said.

"Heck yeah. I've seen people out here swimming for years. I once caught a sunfish in the pond. I threw it back because I knew my mom would never let me cook it up for dinner. You know, I hate my mother for shit like that."

"I love to fish."

"Me too. I sometimes fantasize living in a cabin on a lonesome lake in Canada dropping acid, eating fish, and drinking beer."

"That would be the life, wouldn't it?"

They were both silent in reflection. The moment was everything he could imagine of heaven—stoned-colored patterns on the brown-green grass and the most beautiful girl in the world by his side. Together they shared pastoral bucalia.

"Well," Christa said. She undid the tie on her blouse and revealed a bra underneath. She reached behind her with both hands, unfastening it, letting the bra drop down to the ground, and revealing her round, perfect breasts. A shiver raced through Stephen's body. "Eat a peach," he thought. He knew he had to control his excitement or he'd feel like a fool. He immediately started thinking about batting orders of championship baseball teams. Over the past five years, he had memorized lineups, batting averages, homeruns, and RBI totals from every pennant winner from the sixties. It turned out to be a successful technique to control emotions. He figured it out at summer camp several years back when a counselor humiliated him in front of other campers. He was ready to break down and cry but started going through the 1967 St. Louis Cardinals' batting order— Lou Brock, Curt Flood, Roger Maris, Orlando Cepeda—all the way to the pitcher's spot. It forced the tears back down.

Stephen took his T-shirt off as Christa unbuttoned her shorts. He moved quickly to keep up with her, and then they both pulled down their underwear, and voilà, they were naked.

They looked each other in the eyes, and Christa giggled.

"Last one in's a rotten egg," she said.

The two of them stepped off the foot-high bank onto the muddy, rocky bed beneath the water. It was not nearly as cold as Stephen had imagined. The long summer days had heated it up, and the two of them carefully waded forward.

"I hope we don't step on any crawdads," Christa said.

They continued forward as the water rose to their waist. When it approached Christa's torso, Stephen had to fight the temptation to glance over and take a quick last look down at her bush; instead, he would be a gentleman and look into her eyes. She was staring at him with a knowing smile on her face but said nothing. She simply dove forward and began swimming toward the middle of the pond. Stephen followed suit. The two of them stopped after about ten yards. The pond was deep, and they began treading water, staring at each other and smiling. For the first time since they had been out there, Stephen became aware of the reeling sound of crickets all around them.

"Come here," Christa said.

He was only a few feet away from her but dog-paddled closer. Christa pulled him to her and gave him a kiss on his lips. They stared into the infinity of each other's eyes.

Orlando Cepeda, Tim McCarver, Julián Javier—

Without a moment's notice, Christa pushed herself away from him and began swimming back toward the bank of the pond where they had jumped in. As soon as she could stand up in the water, she turned to him and said, "Come on; let's dry off and smoke some more."

"That was quick," Stephen said. They both laughed

Stephen swam toward her, and the two of them waded back to the grassy bank. The sun poured down on their naked bodies as Christa laid their clothes out like a picnic blanket and sat down.

"We'll dry off quickly, don't you think?"

"I'm comfortable."

Christa smiled. "Do you like school?"

"Not really. Do you?"

"Naw, but I don't have to go anymore unless I go home."

"Are you ever going back?"

"No. My parents want to put me away."

"Away? You mean like here at Montgomery?"

"No, away like an asylum."

"You're kidding."

"No, I'm not."

Christa arched herself up off the ground and slid a hand underneath her butt. She reached into the front pocket of her shorts, which were damp from the water dripping off of her. She pulled out a sloppily folded envelope with a handwritten address on it. She reached inside and slid out the letter that was creased like the envelope, opened it and handed it to Stephen.

"It's a letter to my father from his old college roommate, who's a psychiatrist."

Stephen looked down at it. It was written on professional stationery, but instead of being typed, it was handwritten and difficult to read.

Dear Garrison,

It was so great to meet with you at Scotsmoor last week. I truly value the rare times we get to golf together and reminisce. Sometimes, I think the days when we were becoming what we are were more fun than being it.

I am honored that you entrusted me to meet and evaluate your daughter Christa. She is quite a beautiful young woman and, as you noted, very intelligent—possibly a handicap for her.

I regret to advise you that, in my professional opinion, she is suffering from what we call Borderline Personality Disorder. While not precisely a form of schizophrenia, we believe that it is a threatening condition that, if not treated intensely, can lead to a more permanent mental illness. Some of the common and more dangerous symptoms of BPD in teenagers is the use of marijuana and alcohol as well as sexual promiscuity, both of which we know have played a part in her academic and social decline over the past two and a half years.

It is my recommendation that she be placed in a hospital for long-term observation and treatment for her illness.

Please do not be disconcerted by this suggestion. It is not a moral issue or matter of shame. The medical fraternity is gaining clarity in our understanding of mental illness. We now see that it affects a far greater and more unlikely strata of society. The good news is, in the 1970s, it's more treatable than ever before through a combination of medications and psychotherapy.

The letter went on to provide detailed information on a hospital that the doctor was affiliated with and was signed:
Your dear friend,

Howard (MD)

Stephen was fascinated by the diagnosis "borderline." It made him think of the barren lakes of Ontario just north of Minnesota at the Canadian border. His brother, John-John, took him camping up on Caribou Lake two summers before, and it was there that he took his first acid trip. John-John committed suicide two months later at Reid College in Portland. Since then Stephen had always pictured John-John living up on the borderline.

"I stole it from the mailbox the day it arrived," Christa said, "and that's when I packed my things and took off."

She began pulling her clothes out from underneath her and putting them on. Just a few moments in the hot sun and the water had disappeared off her body. Now her body disappeared into her clothing.

A smile came across Stephen's face as he handed the letter back to Christa. She smiled back at him while he put on his underwear, but behind her smile, he could see a world of deep fear and guilt. He pulled on his jeans as he gazed into her lost eyes.

"Hey," he said, "you'll be OK. The borderline is where all the great sages hang out."

"Aw," Christa said, "I'm no sage. I've done bad things—secrets that I've never told anyone, not even Tyler."

"I know. I can see that in you. It's what really turns me on about you."

Stephen realized he was making a confession and blushed. "I guess that's one of *my* secrets."

Christa smiled, "That's not a secret. I've known you liked me for a while." She leaned in and kissed him on the cheek, letting her naked breast touch his chest. She then strapped on her bra as he pulled his T-shirt over him.

"I have *real* secrets, Stephen. I've done bad things."

"Have you ever killed anybody?"

"No. Have you?"

"No. So, what can be so bad?"

"I'm just ashamed, is all."

"Well you don't have to be ashamed with me. I'm not your dad or your psychiatrist."

Christa giggled for a moment, and then her face straightened up.

"A lot of times I wish I could kill myself, so if people ever found out about the 'real' me, they'd know how much I regretted who I am. That's one of my secrets."

"You know what?" Stephen said. "Last fall in English class, we read this story by Willa Cather. It's called 'Paul's Case.' It's about a kid who's our age who jumps in front of a train and kills himself."

"Oh. I *love* that story!"

"Sometimes when I'm really sad, I fantasize that I'm Paul."
"Oh my God, me too!"

They both stood up involuntarily and started walking back toward the railroad tracks. Their shirts were still moist, and he could see the slight pinkish imprint of Christa's left nipple showing through her bra and blouse. His eyes got stuck there until she gently hit him on the side of the head.

"Hey, what are you lookin' at?"
"Sorry."
"Oh don't be. I was just kidding."
She put her arm around him, and he reciprocated as they

walked up toward the fence between the ranch and the gully beside the railroad bed.

"Don't you wish we could just escape, Stephen? Go far away somewhere."

"Yeah, I do."

The two of them walked along the tracks toward a signal light that stood about a quarter mile to the north. As they walked, a break in the trees to their left revealed a soybean field in the distance where Stephen and his friends liked to hide out during the fall semester. They called it "Barney's Beanery" after a rock and roll album cover by Big Brother and the Holding Company. Farther out, beyond the bean field, on Interstate 94, was a giant twenty-four-hour rest-stop complex on a bridge over the tollway. It was called The Oasis and had gas stations and gift shops on each side and a Fred Harvey's restaurant in the middle overlooking the six-lane highway. The steady flash of the green Fred Harvey sign over the tollway reminded drivers they were on a journey. Sometimes Stephen and his classmates would sneak up there in the wee hours of the morning and have breakfast and buy cigarettes from the machine. They would be tripping on acid—travelers themselves—and as he'd sit overlooking the highway, his imagination would be fired by places to go. Once at exactly midnight, the restaurant's piped-in radio played Maria Muldaur's "Midnight at the Oasis."

Now, walking along the railroad tracks with Christa, his imagination was fired beyond return.

Stephen pointed up the tracks to the signal light.

"The freight trains all slow down to a crawl here because they're so long and there's a sharp curve up at that light. Whenever a train slows down, I think of how easy it would be to jump on a boxcar and go out West."

"I'd love to go out West, Stephen."

They locked gazes again, and he felt the first certainty of his entire life as Christa smiled at him.

"Let's go back to the dorm and grab our stuff," she said.

They walked down off the grade and onto the prep school campus. They wound their way past the smelly pipes and pump house of a water treatment facility until they came to a flower garden behind Montgomery Hall. As they stepped through the garden, Christa reached down and broke a red carnation off a bush. She stuck it into the pocket of Stephen's T-shirt.

"This is in honor of Paul," she said and leaned in to kiss him.

The dorm was empty when they got back. Stephen went into his room and grabbed a small carrying bag and stuffed two pairs of jeans, shirts, socks, and underwear inside, along with his toothbrush, toothpaste, and a comb. He added his pipe, rolling papers, and stash of weed. When he got to the common room, Christa was waiting for him, wearing a little backpack.

"If you have extra stuff, I got room in my pack," she said.

"I'll be OK. I'm just worried about money. I only have thirty dollars."

Christa reached into her pocket and pulled out a roll of hundred dollar bills. Stephen gasped.

"Where did you get that?"

"Like I said, I've done some bad things."

The two of them retraced their steps through the water treatment area and out to the tracks. The hike up to the signal light took about ten minutes.

"I've never bothered to memorize when the different trains run," Stephen said, "but it's really important that we keep our bags hidden when the engine passes, or the engineer will radio the railroad cops, and they'll come kick our ass."

"How do you know all this, Stephen?"

"Because I talk to drifters whenever I see them."

"Me too. And I talk to runaways."

Stephen opened up his carryall and pulled out some rolling papers and his bag of pot. He didn't have time to shake out the seeds, so he rolled the weed in the paper with the fingers of his right hand, pushing the seeds out with his thumb as they rose to his fingertips. He let the powder drop back down into the paper while the seeds and stems fell to the ground. He repeated the process a couple of times, until the paper was full. He rolled it up, licked the glue, and had a perfect joint. All the while Christa watched with reverie.

They sat with their backs against the concrete platform of the signal light and shared the joint. Her head rested on his shoulders, and he reached his arm around her. After about ten minutes they were asleep. Fifteen minutes later they were awakened by an approaching horn and looked down the track and saw the single headlight of a Milwaukee Road freight engine coming toward them. Their bags were tucked safely behind the signal light, hidden from the view of the engineer.

"This is it," he said.

Christa leaned in and gave him a half dozen sloppy kisses on his cheek. Finally, his passion broke loose, and he got an erection.

"Act cool, like we're just hanging out, and wave to

the engineer."

They smiled and waved as the train approached, and the engineer gave a couple of friendly toots from the horn. During the approach, the train decelerated to a walking pace.

Stephen had them wait until about twenty or so cars went by, and then they started walking along beside the train as it passed them on the far side of the curve.

"When I start running, you start running," he said. "We have to pick a car with doors open on both sides so we don't get locked in. I'll throw my bag in and jump on, and then you do the same."

They walked along, slowly letting cars pass them until he found one he liked. He began sprinting ahead of it and threw his bag inside. Before he knew it, he was pulling himself up inside the boxcar. The carnation flew out of his pocket and out onto the bed of the tracks. A moment later a backpack bounced up next to him, and an outstretched arm reached in. He grabbed it and dragged Christa up and along the floor of the car. She pulled herself to her knees. After catching their breath, they sat beside each other cross-legged, looking out at the vast Bannockburn farm, with its milk cows and bulls grazing in pastoral bucolia among the trees. There was a white barn and silo about a half mile in the distance. As the train picked up speed, the Bannockburn Ranch quickly turned into northern Illinois countryside, where flat, empty farmland would soon melt into Wisconsin lakes and trees.

Once again they locked eyes, and Christa let go a euphoric smile like she had finally been rescued from her nightmare and was home at last. Stephen beheld before him his haloed companion, who would join him out on the borderline somewhere between Minnesota and Seattle. Wherever they landed, they would meet up with their own kind and finally be free.

ATTACK OF THE POKER FACE

I knew she was lying; I'd beaten her at poker a hundred times. Camille had this little tell with her left nostril whenever she was bluffing. This, though, was the first time I had ever seen it while we were engaged in regular conversation. Of course, it was also the first time the subject of cheating had ever come up. In retrospect, when we were taking our wedding vows at Saint Clair's Church, I thought I saw her nostril twitching then too.

I was sitting across the street at the Stomping Grounds Café near Twenty-Fourth and Noe in the early afternoon reading a new book on Texas Hold'em. It was a lovely, sun-strewn San Francisco day. People don't know that the city's Mission District area is typically sunny during summertime while the rest of the city bathes in fog. It's actually a fairly temperate climate.

My boss had rewarded me with the afternoon off after I had worked on an intense planning project over the weekend followed by an insufferable two-hour negotiation with city bureaucrats. This was the first time I had spent a nonholiday weekday afternoon away from work since I was in my early twenties. I mean, yeah, I had occasional vacation time off, but Camille and I always spent it in Las Vegas.

I guess what I'm trying to say is, I already felt a little awkward being out on the streets during a weekday. It felt like I was playing hooky from school or trying to score drugs—my sensitivity level was sky-high. So when I looked out the café window and saw Camille across the street in the grips of some other guy, flares of anger shot out from my brain and burned the back of my eyeballs. She was wearing her most expensive designer jeans—the ones she only wears when she's feeling wild and important—and he was in a silk suit with his left hand gently touching her waist as he opened the door of Sushi Sam's.

A sideways gravity pulled me up out of my seat and out the café door into the Twenty-Fourth Street traffic and then across the street to the front window of the Japanese restaurant. Everyone inside looked up at me as I stared through the glass, searching for Camille and her blond, curly-haired escort. I felt like one of those grubby winos who stops at a restaurant window and starts picking his nose in an exaggerated way to make all the diners nauseous. The only people in the entire restaurant who didn't notice me immediately were Camille and her dude. Their eyes were engaged in a lovers' lock. Finally, all the attention I was attracting from the other patrons somehow swept over to them, and they glanced up to see what was going on.

That was Camille's first tell.

Even at a distance, I could see her left nostril widening and shrinking as she looked at me in shock. The businessman dude had his back to the window at first, but he turned around quickly in response to Camille's gape-mouthed expression. Her shock turned to anger as she stood up from the table, where their freshly laid menus had been ignored while they gazed into the sex chambers of each other's eyes. She pushed down the aisle of the restaurant with mad intent past other late luncheoners and burst out the front door.

"Teddy, what on earth are you doing here?" She was blaming me for whatever was wrong with the picture.

"What am *I* doing here?"

"That's what I said. Are you following me?"

"Should I be?"

"Answer my question, Theodore."

"Oh, so now it's *Theodore*."

I borrowed that line from the movie *Casa Blanca*—"Oh, so now it's *Richard*."

"I'm here," I said, "because Mr. Simpson gave me the afternoon off for all the good work I've been doing lately. On the way home, I thought I'd get some coffee at the Stomping Grounds, you know, *our* café. And low and behold, what do I see but some jock-brained hunk with his arm around you, squeezing your ass and taking you out to lunch."

The truth was, the guy didn't look much like a jock, and he never really squeezed her ass—at least not while I was watching—but the whole situation demanded some dramatic elocution on my part.

"Nobody's squeezing anybody's ass, Ted. The only ass here is you. I'm simply having lunch with an old college classmate." At that moment I would have felt like a total fool had it not been for Camille's left nostril. It began doing the bluff dance, opening and closing like an agitated horse.

"You're lying! I know you're lying."

"Oh come on, Ted! Grow up! You're paranoid." Passersby began staring at us as a bona fide scene developed on the front sidewalk.

"You don't think I know when you lie? How do you think I beat the shit out of you at poker all these years? I know when you're bluffing. If he's just a classmate, why don't you take me in and introduce me to him?"

"I'm not going to put Sydney through any discomfort just because I have a paranoid husband."

"How is it paranoid, Camille? Everything is cut-and-dried here. Just like every time you fold before I can look at your cards."

"Is everything poker to you?"

She asked that question a lot. I suddenly realized it was another tell.

I pushed past her into the restaurant. I plowed down the aisle but managed to put a big plastic smile on my face.

"Hi, Sydney!" I said. "I'm Ted, Camille's husband. Such a surprise seeing you here."

Sydney shrank in his seat. He had gone from tall, handsome, and self-assured to a shivering Chihuahua.

"I . . . this . . . Camille said you were at work . . ."

"Sydney," said Camille, who was now standing behind me, "don't say another word!" She knew my poker prowess and could see I had this idiot pegged by every stupid word that stuttered forth from his mouth.

He sat up and squeezed himself out of the red leather booth. "I'm really sorry." He was pleading for clemency, probably expecting me to punch him in the nose. He turned to Camille. "Honey . . . I mean, Camille. I need to leave now." With that he turned and dashed out of the restaurant.

A little Japanese man in a sports jacket walked up to us and asked, "Is there a problem here, Ms. Heatherhorn?"

"No," Camille said quickly. "Everything's fine, Sam."

I couldn't believe it. They knew each other by name. In all the time we had been together, Camille had never mentioned that she was a regular at Sushi Sam's.

"What, is *every*body in on this little secret?"

"Ted, stop it. There's no secret." Her left nostril was now dilating like a birth canal.

I turned to Sam. "This is my wife, Camille. Congratulations! Your little sushi hut is ground zero for my wife's adultery. I bet that makes you feel good. How many other cheating couples do you have here?"

The restaurant was silent save for a Death Cab for Cutie song on the sound system, "Follow You into Hell" or something. There was the smell of teriyaki sauce and fried tempura in the air. The customers were all looking up at us. Their attention seemed to be centered on Sushi Sam; they were hoping for guidance, I suppose.

"Any other cheaters in the house?" I called out. I knew this would get me kicked out, but I also knew I had shamed Camille, and she'd have no choice but to leave with me.

I started walking up and down the aisle to the tables against the wall. "Any adultery going on here? Any gals playing the field while you're dopey husbands are off at work?" I stopped at a table where an adorable redhead was sitting with a nerdy, computer-type guy.

"Oh come on, doll," I said. "You can do better than that. Hell, I could surely find you a hotter ticket. How 'bout that blond, curly haired hunk who just left my wife? He's available now. I bet you can get some good nooky there!"

Camille pushed past me and stormed out of the restaurant. Sam was now quite distraught. "Sir, I'm going to have to ask you to leave."

"It's *Mr. Heatherhorn*!" I said. "If you can call my wife Ms. Heatherhorn, you can call me mister."

"Yes, yes of course, Mr. Heatherhorn. Now please leave."

I turned and walked out.

I looked down Twenty-Fourth to Castro Street and saw Camille sitting on a bus stop bench sobbing. An old couple was sitting alongside her, staring with sympathetic eyes. I walked over and stood in front of her.

She looked up. "Go away! Haven't you done enough?" Her nostril was no longer flickering.

The gray-haired old lady gave me a fierce glance. "Have some mercy on this woman."

I looked over to her husband as I pointed at the old lady. "Has she ever cheated on you? How would you feel if you saw your wife with a hot stud going into a raw fish store across the street?"

"Why, I'd think I had better open my eyes and find out what I'm doing wrong." The old lady put her hand on his knee and patted it. Camille leaned into her as the old woman put her other arm around Camille's shoulder.

So it was going to be this way. She had engaged a ringer to do her bluffing. I turned around and walked home.

MONKEY BUSINESS

The field was horrible with blood, bashed skulls, and Louisville Slugger baseball bats. The baseball bats were strewn through the carnage of seven dead children. Even for India, which had seen its share of violence, this was a bona fide bloodbath.

Little Timmy Thompson—broken and trembling—tried to explain what had happened to a Madhapar city policeman interviewing him. Timmy was the primary witness to the worst massacre ever seen in that wealthy community in Western India near the Arabian Gulf. The appearance of the bodies and blood-stained field gave every indication of a horrid terrorist attack.

Timmy stood over the corpse of his beloved father, the Reverend Dirk Thompson, who came to India with the most sincere intentions in his heart.

"Tell me everything you saw, young sir," said the handsome, dark-skinned police officer, who spoke English like an Indian scholar.

"Daddy only wanted to do right," Timmy said.

The policeman was momentarily mortified as he looked around at the carnage. "You mean *your father* did this?"

"No! No sir, not at all. He tried to stop it. Heck, he tried to *prevent* it. He saw all this coming yesterday, during morning practice."

Poor Timmy couldn't hold his brave, stone face—he burst into tears. Afa'sar, the policeman, attempted to console the boy by rubbing his shoulder while other officers sifted through the ruins out on the freshly mowed field.

A small crowd was developing, and there was only one other remaining survivor left at the scene, a child wearing blood-stained clothes, sitting and crying just a few feet from a chalk line that the Reverend Dirk had carefully drawn that morning. It was one of two straight white lines at a ninety-degree angle that extended exactly three hundred feet from a white, pentagon-shaped rubber disk on the ground.

"Who exactly is your father?" said the Indian, standing at attention in his khaki uniform. He looked down again at the dead man dressed in black, with a white minister's collar stained in blood. There were deep, gaping, gashes in the man's forehead.

"He's a Southern Baptist minister from Arkansas, sir. And an avid baseball fan too. He came here to bring baseball—I mean *quality* baseball—to India. He had read so much about your people, sir. You know, your rapid growth and industrialization. That's what Daddy said, '*industrialization*.' I guess that means like factories and computers and stuff. He said you guys were 'embracing the Western ways,' and we needed to help you."

"I don't understand."

"Baseball, sir. Pop wanted to teach you baseball. He wanted to create an Olympic-quality baseball team that India could be proud of. He said it would lead to a religious awakening."

"We have baseball in this town, son. In fact we even have

a field, one of the only in India, not more than a mile east of here. But you must understand, we prefer cricket. It's the game of our British cousins."

"We were at that field," Timmy said. The memory stirred more sobbing. "There were wild monkeys. That's how the whole thing started, sir. With the monkeys."

"Yes, I understand that. Please go on, son. I know this is difficult." Afa'sar himself could barely hold his emotions as he looked at the brain matter oozing out of the minister's head.

Timmy was sniffling but continued. "Well, originally we started playing over at another field—we call it a 'diamond.' It was the day before yesterday, but at eleven o'clock, a pack of monkeys showed up and ripped apart the big bag full of salami sandwiches and sodas that dad had brought to help the Indian boys celebrate their first day of practice. The boys were so excited to be there! A real, *live* American baseball coach!

"Anyway, I don't know what got into Pop, but he became livid. 'I'll kill those sons of bitches,' he said. Daddy had a temper, and those monkeys looked pretty mean. Pop said they were evil."

Timmy settled down—his words seemed to evoke a fond memory from childhood.

"I saw him get like that once before—in our backyard in Arkansas with some raccoons. He grabbed a shotgun and chased them till he found their nest, and then he killed them all. Pop was so good with a gun!"

Afa'sar tried hard to hold back his horror as the kid spoke.

"Of course, he couldn't bring his rifle or pistol with him on the trip here. They won't allow 'em on airplanes on account of terrorists and all. But he was determined to get even with the monkeys.

"Harjeet . . ." Timmy pointed to the dead body next to the pitcher's mound, "said the monkeys came to town looking for food every morning around eleven o'clock and that the safest thing Daddy could do was keep the sandwiches in metal lunch boxes. Harjeet had a bunch of lunch boxes at home 'cause he was from a big family, and all his brothers and sisters brought their lunches to school. Daddy shook his head in disgust. When we got back to our boarding house, he told me Harjeet was a 'coward' who wasn't capable of being a good pitcher. Daddy said he knew that type—a 'pacifist.' He would never be able to brush back a hitter crowding the plate. Pop taught me long ago that if you couldn't throw a fastball dead on at an opposing bat-ter, you had no business playing the game. I guess he learned that from somewhere in the Bible.

"Anyways, the next morning—that was yesterday—Dad-dy had a plan. At ten o'clock, Pop brought our baseballs and twelve Louisville Slugger baseball bats back to that other dia-mond across town again. The number twelve was for the orig-inal apostles of Jesus. There was twelve of 'em until Judas went all berserk. Then there were only eleven.

"My job was to be the catcher; I tossed all the baseballs on the ground next to Harjeet on the pitcher's mound and crouched behind the plate while Daddy batted. Like I said, this was over at the other diamond."

"Yes, exactly," said Afa'sar. "The one on Pandavi Road. It's also a cricket field. It's very popular."

While Afa'sar was talking, a cop out in the middle of the field waved another officer over to point out a boy's fractured spine. The crowd was getting larger, and a mother screamed as she ran out to look for her child in the carnage.

Timmy was barely holding on. He was pale and looked like he might get sick, but he continued.

"Harjeet was on the mound," he said, "and Daddy hit grounders to the infielders, who tossed them over to first base. And then, between groundballs, Dad would hit fly balls to the outfielders. The boys were having a hard time judging flies at first but got better really fast. It was a sight to behold."

Timmy looked up to heaven in reverie. Then he looked back down at his father again and back at Afa'sar. He looked away trying to remember more details of the previous day. "After each play, they'd throw the ball to me at home, and I'd throw it back to Harjeet."

"Well, it sounds like a lot of fun," said Afa'sar. Another officer called out to him in Hindi to come over and look at something.

"Not now!" Afa'sar yelled in English. "I'm interviewing a witness."

"Anyway," Timmy continued, "just before eleven, Pop called one of the outfielders in." Timmy pointed over to the left at another dead child, this one drenched in his own blood, which was oozing out along the third-base chalk line. "He had him up at the plate batting. Daddy told me to stay put while he grabbed a bat and disappeared into some bushes in front of a grove of trees behind the backstop."

Afa'sar nodded. He knew those bushes well. Sometimes Indian teenagers would hang out in that grove at night and drink beers.

"Well, sure enough, at eleven o' clock a bunch of monkeys came out of nowhere like in the Wizard of Oz—that's a movie we kids watch back home—and Daddy rushed out of the bushes with his bat and really nailed one of 'em in the skull, knocking it to the ground. Then he just wailed on it until it was dead. All the other monkeys started to run away, but then they stopped and looked back at the dead one. It was like they were in mourning or something, but all the time they seemed to be studying the scene and trying to figure out what happened."

Timmy looked off in the distance, as if watching a John Wayne movie. "So, Pop yells out to the monkeys: 'See? This is what happens in America if you steal people's lunches, you *mother . . .*' I can't repeat the word Pop said because it's bad, but still, I can understand Daddy saying it as angry as he was and all.

"All the kids came running in. They'd never seen anything like it—a dead monkey with its skull smashed in. Daddy told me Indians opened monkey skulls and ate their brains out, but we found out later at our boarding house that that was the Chinese.

"Anyway, the kids were freaked, and Pop had to cancel practice for the day. After practice we had a taxi driver take us around town until we found this field here. Daddy had me call Harjeet and set up today's workout. We chalked up the baselines and the foul lines and laid out the bases before the boys arrived. It was like a *field of dreams*."

"OK, Timmy. Tell me exactly what happened today."

Timmy started bawling. He was shaking uncontrollably and Afa'sar was ready to release him to an ambulance to be taken to the hospital. Afa'sar rubbed Timmy's shoulders again and pulled the boy's head to his side. "Be brave, boy. You can do it; you can tell me."

"Well it was like this: Daddy moved us over to this field because he didn't want to mess with the monkeys after the scene yesterday. He spent the first hour with a bat in hand, coaching the boys out in the field. That way if any monkeys showed up, he could club 'em." Timmy pointed over to the sandwiches, which were in a big, clear plastic bag about twenty feet from the third baseline. The stream of blood from the dead third baseman had reached and stained the corner of the bag.

"By eleven fifteen, nothing bad happened, so Daddy put his bat over by the fence with all the others and called for batting practice. One by one, the boys were supposed to come up to the plate to bat. When it was someone's turn to hit, I would fill in for him out in the field. Harjeet was pitching, and the first batter up was Jagdesh, the left fielder."

Timmy looked toward the horizon as if he was hallucinating or visualizing a nightmare. He stood frozen, unable to speak for several seconds, but then started up again excitedly.

"As I stood out in left field, I saw them coming. There were eleven of 'em; they came from out of the weeds behind home plate." Timmy pointed to the tall grass behind the makeshift batter's box.

"It was horrible! I saw them and I yelled. '*Daddy, Daddy!*' but he must of thought I was being hysterical. He used to always say I was hysterical. I never believed him, but now I wish I had, so he'd have believed me.

"One of the monkeys ran up to the bats, grabbed a handful

and started handing them out to the other monkeys until all eleven of them had a bat in their little monkey hands. And then . . ."

Timmy was bawling—gargling through his tears. "They went on a rampage. They started with Daddy. Two of them jumped in front of him, and as he was fending them off, a third jumped on his back from behind and with his free hand, started clubbing Daddy until his head cracked open." Timmy fell to the ground and crawled over to his father's body through a pool of dark blood. He looked up at the field of dead children.

"And then they went to town on the rest of the kids. Us three in the outfield were able to run off, but one of the monkeys threw a bat and hit Lakshmana, the right fielder, on the side of his face, and now he's all bloodied up, but the two of us got out of there. When we got to the street, the monkeys were gone."

As Timmy finished, another policeman walked up and addressed Afa'sar.

"I've never seen anything like this."

"It was the monkeys," Afa'sar said.

"I know; we talked to the other boy. The monkeys were provoked," said the policeman as he pointed to Reverend Dirk Thompson lying dead on the ground. He tried to speak softly, but Timmy heard him.

"No they weren't! Daddy tried to stop 'em. He hated the monkeys; if he'd had his shotgun he would have killed 'em all."

"Now, now, Timmy," said Afa'sar. "We're not casting blame."

Timmy screamed. "Why couldn't Daddy kill the monkeys?"

Afa'sar got down on his knees next to Timmy and began rubbing his shoulders.

"Son, I'm sure your father and all these boys are in a better place now. Maybe he and his lord Jesus can teach them baseball up in heaven."

As the two of them knelt, a series of ambulances and coroner's cars came streaming up to the field. It had been determined that there were no other survivors left on the field except the other surviving outfielder, who was now being escorted from the scene in an ambulance. A second ambulance had rolled up onto the grass and backed up to the chalk line, twenty feet away from Afa'sar and Timmy. Two Indian paramedics dressed all in white hopped out and opened the backdoor and pulled a gurney out of the back of the truck. They rolled it up to Timmy, and Afa'sar stood up and gently lifted him onto it.

"We need to go to the hospital and make sure you're OK."

"I'm OK. They didn't touch me. I want to stay with my daddy."

"We need to take your father out of here, son; this is no place to be. The medical examiner will look at him, and then we can make plans for you and the rest of your family."

Afa'sar put his arm around Timmy and then turned and faced him and lifted the gurney. The paramedics strapped him in.

"I'll see you at the hospital, Timmy."

An hour later Afa'sar walked into the emergency room and found Timmy strapped to a bed as he lay crying. He walked up to Timmy and put his hand through his hair but could offer no words of condolence. What was there to say?

After a few moments, Timmy looked up at the ceiling. "Why, Jesus? Why? Daddy killed the raccoons. Why couldn't Daddy kill the monkeys?"

THE DOBERMAN AFFAIR

Freddy Haskin was okay with dogs; in fact he liked 'em—most of them at least. Little Chihuahuas and wiener dogs were rather grotesque and seemed to have a higher percentage of dander to fur. All in all, though, dogs were a happy thing, and Freddy liked happy things. Freddy even started liking pit bulls as it became more politically correct.

Freddy's wife, Donna Jean, however, was once bitten by a beagle outside a drugstore when she was eight years old and never got over it. Freddy knew the story well—a poor little girl reaches down to pet a pretty doggie on the top of its head, and it suddenly snaps at her like a whip. The next thing you know, she's got puncture marks and blood leaking out of her hand.

"You don't get over a thing like that," Donna said many times.

"No, you don't," Freddy would respond in kindness.

But the truth was, there comes a point when a person has to rise up and transcend life's great injustices. Gandhi tried to teach the world that, and he was also a great animal lover.

"You know," Freddy remarked one evening, "Gandhi said that you can tell a culture by how it treats its dogs." He and

Donna were cuddling on the living room couch in front of a warm, glowing December fireplace. A soft, orange reflection danced upon the walls behind them as they sat serenely in the dark.

"Bullshit!" she said. She jumped off the couch in midcuddle and stormed up to the bedroom. This was the kind of thing that drove Freddy bonkers. Ordinarily, Donna Jean was like a throwback to a 1960s love child. She had age-old hippy sensibilities in all aspects of her life except the dreaded dog thing.

Freddy and Donna had a deep penchant for the sixties. Their moms and dads had lived on a 1960s commune together (it was actually in the mid-70s) in California's magnificent Mendocino County when they were both four years old. The two of them played together on a glorious green, grassy field adjacent to the tomato and zucchini patches.

When Donna turned five, she and her mom were called away from the farm to take care of her grandma. Her dad didn't come along because apparently her mother's family hated him.

After that, Donna and Freddy completely lost touch with each other, but they never forgot. Growing up, they each often recalled the green field, and the vegetable patches, and the chickens, pigs, and cows, and, yes, there were dogs. They loved to play with the dogs—two blond Labrador retrievers and an Irish setter named Big Red.

Freddy's family fled the commune six months after Donna's in a heated dispute over religion and animal sacrifice. Everybody left and went his or her own way. Freddy and Donna Jean met again sixteen years later at Cal Berkeley and got married shortly thereafter.

From these childhood memories, Freddy grew an aversion to conflict. He wanted things to be mellow. Freddy always liked that phrase "happy camper" until he got beat up a couple of times in high school for using it. Getting beat up was not "mellow," so he stashed the phrase away until his thirtieth birthday when, after blowing out the candles on his cake, he turned to Donna and said, "You know what, darling? I'm a happy camper." She kissed him, and they immediately went up to the bedroom and made love.

Unfortunately, the next-door neighbors' brand new "rescue" Doberman pinscher was now changing the layout of Freddy's happy campground. It was a tall, handsome thing that the Barnabys kept on a very long leash out on their back driveway. Their plan was to create a runner tied between two trees in the backyard and hook the dog up and let it have the run of the property to chase chipmunks, hares, and other pests. In the meantime, the blacktopped driveway had to suffice as the maximum expanse of the dog's empire.

The two-year-old Doberman, whom the Barnabys had cleverly named Dobie, had an exceptional skill for moving about the driveway without making a sound. It was almost otherworldly how he did that. He was like that Shaolin priest on the old *Kung Fu* TV show. Even the scraping of his chain on the blacktop was virtually inaudible as he moved in complete Zen-like stealth while he staked out prey. Otherwise, he was your typical goofy, sloppy dog.

One early autumn evening as Donna was taking the trash out to the garbage bin by their garage, she glanced over at the Barnabys' driveway and saw Dobie sleeping by the back steps.

She smiled at the animal gamely as he briefly lifted his head to see if snacks were coming and then went back to sleep. Feeling safe, Donna proceeded with the trash. No more than ten seconds later, as she reached to lift the metal lid off the garbage can, her hand was met by Dobie's cold and curious nose. She screamed and threw the bag up in the air, scattering compost and empty food packages everywhere. The dog began barking ferociously at the misunderstanding but then realized there were items of great interest spewed out upon the ground and left Donna alone so he could scavenge the area.

When Donna described the incident to Freddy, it was followed by the cry, "You have to *do* something! Do something *now* before someone gets killed!"

Freddy was left to contemplate which would be less "mellow," a stealth dog and angry wife or no dog but angry next-door neighbors.

The Barnabys, of course, were well within their rights to own a dog, and the dog was technically on its own property when the trashcan miscommunication took place. In fact, Paul Barnaby had once joked with Freddy that the Haskins' garbage can was technically on his property since it sat on the other side of a narrow dirt path that led behind the garage. Freddy kept the can there because he needed the path open to save time getting to a woodpile for their fireplace.

The woodpile, Paul noted, was half on his property as well, and he would sometimes joke, "So I guess you wouldn't mind if I borrowed some logs for my fireplace now and then. Huh?" Freddy would laugh, and then they'd talk jovially about something else.

Those were the kinds of things that made good neighbors good neighbors. Better even than the fences that Robert Frost wrote about.

As Freddy rang the doorbell on the Barnabys' back door, he rehearsed a little monologue for Paul about loving dogs himself, and how Donna was once bitten, suffering years of deep psychological anguish, and how noble it was for the Barnabys to rescue a Doberman from extinction, and how generous Paul was for letting the trashcans and the woodpile share his property, and so on, but enough was enough.

Paul answered the door with a beer can in his hand.

"Freddy!" he yelled. "You don't come by enough! You're a goddamn neighbor for Christ's sake! How the hell are you?"

Dobie the Doberman immediately came prancing to the door and pushed his snout directly into Freddy's crotch in a way that, awkward in itself, felt even more perilous by the presence of his notorious Doberman teeth and jaws.

"Isn't that cute," Paul said. He was genuinely gleeful about Dobie's discovery of Freddy's privates.

Freddy looked down at the dog's nose pressed deep into his blue jeans. Dobie was wearing a tie-dyed scarf around his neck.

"Check out Dobie's hippy scarf," Paul said. "Joan and I bought it especially for you guys! We know how much you and Donna dig all that hippy jazz and thought it would make Dobie feel like your dog too. Come on in!"

"No, no. I just wanted to talk for a quick sec, Paul."

"No, the Auburn-Ohio State game is on. If you want to talk, it'll be in front of the TV with a beer in your hand."

"Well, OK. I can do that."

He enunciated the "I can do that" in such a way that it sounded like he was simply saying he was *capable* of doing that. Paul led him through the back hallway past the kitchen and out through their immaculate, plush white living room into their not-so-immaculate, wood-paneled den. There was an empty lounge chair in front of a blaring TV that Paul said was "begging" for Freddy's presence. The TV was now screaming about an interception.

"Oh shit!" Paul said as he tried to figure out what had just happened. "Please be Auburn, please be Auburn. Oh God, please make it Auburn."

"Please be Auburn what?" Freddy asked.

"*Yes*! An Auburn interception on their twenty-yard line."

Paul walked over to a bar across the room with a minifridge on it. He opened the refrigerator door and said, "I hope you like Miller's. That's all we drink here."

"Sure. A Miller's would be fine."

"Oh, that's right. You like that snob shit."

"Corona is *not* snob shit, Paul."

"Whatever. It's Mexican sludge."

"Yeah, I guess."

"I was just kidding, you know."

"Sure."

"They should just open the borders and pack this country full of Mexicans. They can eat all our corn and take all our jobs. Sons of bitches."

Freddy nodded his head nervously. He wanted to somehow steer the conversation away from Mexicans and over to Dobie the Doberman.

"Fucking Chihuahuas," Freddy said out of nowhere.

"Hey! What the fuck's the matter with Chihuahuas?"

"Oh nothing, if you're bilingual."

"Hey, knock off the Chihuahua thing. They're innocent victims of this whole immigration issue."

"So anyway, I wanted to talk about Dobie."

At the sound of his name, Dobie the Doberman came charging into the room from his favorite spot on the white living room couch.

"Isn't that the greatest thing you've ever seen?" Paul said. "They talk about Jack Russells being smart, but look at this!"

Dobie immediately skipped over to Freddy's lounge chair and pushed his legs open with his head and stuck his nose back into Freddy's crotch.

"Paul, come on! Could you give me a break?"

"Just yell at him! Tell him to knock it off."

Freddy looked down and caught a side glimpse of Dobie's sharp teeth and pink gums as his nose continued to push inward.

"Uh, Dobie," Freddy said. Dobie's eyes rolled up at him. "Stop it. OK, pup?"

"*Dobie! Get the fuck out of here!* Git, boy!"

The dog looked up at Paul, whimpered briefly, and then turned and romped out through the living room toward the back hallway. Freddy could hear the sound of the dog's paws pushing up and clawing on the back screen door.

"So here's the thing, Paul. Donna Jean had a bit of an incident when she was eight years old." Freddy realized that he had made a pun and laughed.

Paul laughed. "What kind of incident?"

"Well, she was bit by a beagle outside a corner drugstore in Orange County."

"Fucking beagles!"

"Yes, well the point is, it kind of messed with her. And . . ."

"A *bit* of an incident! Ha! I get it! That's hysterical!"

"Paul, it messed her head up! She's never been quite the same around dogs."

"Oh, that's too bad. It must be hard for you."

"Yeah, kind of."

"Winston Churchill once said, 'A woman who doesn't like dogs will be proven a fool.'"

"Did he really?"

"Yup."

"Well the point is . . ."

"Men are kind of like dogs, you know what I mean?"

"Not really."

"Well, we're loyal and loving, but we do like to play hard and sometimes . . ."

The TV blared out, "*Caught at the Ohio State sixteen-yard line!*"

Paul jumped up out of his chair and then raised his beer can to toast Freddy. "Those boys are going all the way! You know what I mean?"

"Yes, I do. Listen, Paul." Freddy had to speak over the din of the crowd noises on the TV. "Donna's a little freaked out by Dobie, I have to tell you."

Paul immediately grabbed the remote and lowered the volume on the TV set.

"Why? What's going on? What did Dobie do?"

"Nothing. It smelled her hand when she was putting the

garbage out, and she freaked out."

"Freddy, that's what dogs do. They smell things."

"She says the dog snuck up on her."

"What, like a prowler? It's his own property. He can go where he chooses so long as the chain goes that far."

"The chain is actually too long for your driveway. The dog could . . . *accidentally* . . . step into our drive and . . . well . . . I just would hate for there to be an ugly situation."

"*Ugly* situation? You mean you're gonna sue Dobie for trespassing?"

"No, not at all. I was hoping maybe you could do something. I mean now, before you get too attached to the thing."

"What are you suggesting?"

Paul's face turned red. Suddenly the TV, now at a soft volume, blared out, "Touchdown, Auburn!" Paul grabbed the remote and shut it off.

"You bastard! You want to step in between us and our dog?"

"It's not for me. It's for Donna. She—"

"And now you're blaming it on your wife? You stinking, Chihuahua-hating coward!"

"Paul, let's be men about this."

"I see only one man here. Well, I can't really see him 'cause it's me. I want to make something perfectly clear, Fred—the dog stays. I'll shorten the leash if you want, but then you have to move your trash cans and your woodpile. Is that clear?"

There was a deadly silence as Freddy grasped for words. Then the silence was broken by the sound of the back kitchen door being forced open and then, moments later, Dobie howling madly from the driveway out back. Freddy and Paul both jumped out of their chairs and dashed through the living room down the hallway to the back door. When Freddy got outside, he saw Donna lying on her back on the pavement in front of the garbage can with Dobie standing over her. Dobie looked over at Paul and Freddy and immediately ran toward them about halfway and then turned and started toward Donna again, looking back at them briefly.

"Jesus Christ," yelled Freddy. "This is exactly what I was talking about."

Donna turned her head to the men and said, "Call an ambulance, please."

They continued toward her as Paul pulled out his cell phone. Freddy began to kneel down to grab her hand and help her up when Dobie snarled at him.

"Oh great. Now I can't get to my dying wife because of your dog!"

"*Dobie! Heal!*" Paul called out.

"That makes no sense," Freddy said. Suddenly he felt a gust of inspiration. "Dobie, *sit down*, damn it!"

The dog sat down beside Donna. Freddy tried to lean in again to reach her, but Dobie snarled at him. Donna looked up at Freddy with tears in her eyes.

"Don't touch me. Don't try to pick me up. Just call an ambulance."

Paul was already talking to a 911 dispatcher. He gave them the address, adding, "And step on it!"

The two men stood and stared down at Donna, who reached her hand out toward Dobie, and he leaned into it and licked it. She was smiling, and Dobie stood up and licked her face. She began petting his head and neck with her right hand.

"My hero," she said and then moaned loudly from the strain. Dobie whimpered.

The two men remained silent as they watched the interchange. A gentle autumn breeze blew through the backyard.

"Honey, everything's gonna be OK," Freddy said. "Paul called an ambulance."

The area around the garage was permeated with the odor of rotten garbage. Freddy looked down at Donna's feet and saw an empty white packet of Green Giant string beans and realized that it had fallen out of the bag, and she had slipped on it and fell on her back. As he noticed this, the sound of a siren broke the silent atmosphere.

Freddy got down on his knees. This time Dobie let him reach out and touch her.

"Don't move me, Fred."

"I know, baby."

The ambulance came rolling up the driveway with its lights flashing. Within moments two paramedics were out of the vehicle and moved Dobie and the men out of the way. They felt around her body and asked her questions while another man came from around the back pushing a gurney.

One of the paramedics looked up at the two men.

"Did you guys find her?"

Without thinking, Freddy said, "The dog did." Then he added, "She's my wife."

"It doesn't look like there's any serious injury to the spine, maybe a few bruised ribs, but I'm not a doctor. She'll get some X-rays at the hospital, and we'll see what happens."

They carefully lifted her onto the gurney that had been laid flat on the ground. They raised it up and began rolling her to the back door of the ambulance. She looked down at Dobie, who was faithfully following the gurney along, and then reached down and let the dog lick her hand again.

"Thank you, sweetie!" she said. "By the way, I like your scarf!"

Freddy looked at Paul with a tear in his eyes, and the two of them shook hands. He pulled out his car keys ready to follow the ambulance to the hospital.

"I guess maybe Winston Churchill was right after all," Freddy said.

"Not really. I made that up."

"Oh hell. I never much cared for Winston Churchill anyway."

"What the fuck's the matter with Winston Churchill?"

"He hated Chihuahuas, Paul."

"Really?"

"Naw, I made that up." Freddy patted Paul on the shoulder and then walked quickly to his car as the sound of the ambulance blared off in the distance.

THE STELLER HUNT

"I wanna bang a beaver."

Merton Callaghan was a crude son of a bitch, though sometimes he made a good point. Still, to blurt that out at Carl's Jr. with people on either side of them made Conrad uncomfortable. He looked around, trying to size up any potential embarrassment from the neighboring tables and see if, in fact, he even knew anybody there. When he was satisfied that nobody was listening or cared, he responded.

"Yeah, I guess I want to bang one too."

"Well, let's go, buddy. Let's finish our burgers and head over to the Trailhead and find a couple of willing babes."

Conrad had never been on a beaver hunt with anybody. Usually when he picked up a girl, he was by himself, and it was a resignation thing, as in, "Well, I guess we're together here (usually a bar), so we might as well go back to my place and do it." It didn't really matter whose place was "my place," at least not to Conrad. But to go out with another guy to find a pair of willing girls who would be attractive *and* attracted to the two of them seemed a bit far-fetched.

"Is the Trailhead a good place to do that?"

"Hell, yeah. I've gotten lucky there a bunch of times. Hey, maybe we can get a hotel room and bang 'em together. You know, swap."

"I don't know if I like sharing so much." In truth, Conrad was deeply averse to the idea. He had performance issues and hated distraction. A brawny loudmouth like Merton would totally throw him off his beaver-banging game if he even had one.

Merton held up his burger and displayed it to Conrad. It was in a paper wrapper and had ketchup, relish, and melted cheese dripping down the side.

"You know," he said, "there's something about a Carl's Jr. cheeseburger that makes me horny. Do you feel the same way?"

Conrad didn't but said, "Yeah, it's the whole juiciness thing. It really gets me going."

The bright, fast-food fluorescent lights made this burgeoning sex project feel a bit flimsy. Conrad would rather go home and watch a new sci-fi movie that had just premiered on pay-per-view. The Iranian Empire had colonized "The Pluto Triumvirate"—Earth's three nearest and largest planetoids in the Kuiper Belt, which remained in relatively close proximity to one another because of their long orbit around the sun. The Iranians now had complete control over the vast resources of a new and powerful fuel that was being mined in the Kuiper Belt and shipped back to Earth. Meanwhile, American and Israeli crusaders were heading out there to save the solar system for Judeo-Christian democracy.

Banging a beaver was great, but a movie lasted longer, and you didn't have the awkward moment of what to do with it when it was over. Still, Merton was Conrad's best friend, and he wanted to spend some quality time with him to ensure their friendship stayed intact.

"Hey, do we have to go to a bar?" Conrad asked. "I don't really feel like drinking tonight."

"Hell yeah. What did you think; we were gonna go score chicks at the library?"

"Or maybe a café or something?"

"No way! It's the Trailhead. Eat up your burger, buddy boy."

The two of them quickly scarfed down their burgers and fries and sucked up their sodas. Conrad started to grab all the scattered litter on the table to put in the garbage, but Merton stopped him.

"Dude, that's what people get paid for. You're being a labor buster doing shit like that."

Conrad left the wrappers and cups on top of the two trays that he had stacked carefully, and the two of them walked swiftly out of the restaurant into the suburban night lights.

The Trailhead was two blocks down Seventh Street, and Merton walked a little ahead of Conrad, sporting a black leather jacket with his hands in his pocket. It was fifty degrees out and dropping, and Conrad thought he could see a whisper of his breath when he exhaled. When they got to a traffic light, a red Mustang pulled up. Merton looked inside, and his eyes got big. Conrad glanced over to see what caught his attention. Behind the wheel was a gorgeous brunette in a halter-top who was brushing her hair while looking into the rearview mirror, which had been pulled down low so she could see herself. Merton started howling.

"Woof, woof! Woof, woof!" he said like a barking dog.

The woman looked up at him and gave him the finger.

"Aw, come on, sweetie," he begged. "Look at us. We're innocent lambs looking for fun on a Friday night." The light turned green, and she peeled off.

Merton put his arm around Conrad's shoulder. "She doesn't know what she's missing. The two of us would have given her a night she'd never forget."

"I don't doubt it," Conrad said.

The Trailhead had a huge marquee jutting out over the sidewalk with neon lights depicting a big square lasso with whiskey bottles floating around inside next to the words The Trailhead. Below the name, a caption read, Where Studs and Mares Meet.

When Conrad and Merton pushed open the double doors and stepped inside, they were hit with the sounds of an old '60s R&B song on the sound system. It was Smokey Robinson singing, "The Hunter Gets Captured by the Game." Conrad recognized the song because this girl at work, Kelsey, was a huge Motown fan and played the stuff softly at her desk all day. He had grown a strong taste for it, but maybe it was because of Kelsey. She was slender with Goth, bleached-blonde hair, and Conrad would have been happy to bang her beaver but was too polite to ask.

"The place is a little dead," Merton said.

Conrad looked around; there were a good twenty or so people at the bar and three chicks at the pool table. He was unclear what Merton considered dead or alive. Perhaps Merton required a wider spectrum of women to offset the inevitable failure factor.

"Welp," he said, "we'll have to make the best of it, Connie boy."

"Sure. It won't be so bad."

As they stood inside the doorway of the dark barroom, Conrad checked to see if there was anyone he knew there, particularly women. He was nervous about the proposition of hitting on chicks and getting rejected in front of people who might gossip about it. At the corner of the bar he saw one old high school dimwit who wasn't friends with anybody he cared about.

"Well let's get to work," Merton said.

"What do we do?"

"We get drinks—first round's on me. What are you having?"

"White wine, please."

"Oh, fuck that, man—get a beer or a cocktail." He shook his head. "Jesus, Conrad, be a man."

"OK then. I'll take a Bud."

"Atta boy. Get a good 'Bud gleam' going in your eye. Then we'll go over to the pool table and see what those babes are looking for."

"But there's three of them."

"Who gives a shit. One of them is probably a 'prop' anyway."

"A prop?"

"Yeah, she's there to fill out the scene for the two that are looking for fun."

"Which one's the prop?"

"There's only one way to find out."

Conrad walked up to the long wooden bar. It was stained brown with a curved edge and was well worn and faded. Chips were broken off, leaving gouges that had been sanded and buffed, presumably to keep drunks from cutting themselves.

Conrad stood beside Merton at an empty stool, where

Merton ordered a gin and tonic and a Budweiser. Conrad wondered if a gin and tonic might provide a more secure image for barroom beaver hunting. The two of them walked over to the pool table, which was in a back corner of the room. There were several small side tables with chairs along the walls. A couple of tables had jackets and purses scattered around them. Merton placed his cocktail on an empty table a couple of seats down from the girls and looked up at the three of them. They looked back as they giggled and shot one another skeptical glances.

"Can I get in line to play the winner?" he asked.

The three of them giggled some more, and then one of them, a tall blonde with a red cashmere sweater and dark lipstick, stepped forward.

"We're not actually playing, just shooting. But I'll play you after we finish this round. You gotta rack 'em up though."

"That sounds like a plan."

The girls giggled once again. Conrad figured it was because "sounds like a plan" was such a lame and clichéd response.

Conrad sat down at a table farthest from the girls. He took a big swig of his beer, and then Merton reached back, grabbed his gin and tonic and did the same. Merton remained standing as he studied the situation and watched the blonde clean up the table with skill. Merton had the reputation of being a good pool player, but it may have only been because he said he was.

"You're good," Merton said to the blonde. He had throaty lust in his voice, as if being good at pool was analogous to being hot in the sack.

She gave him a mocking sneer as she finished off the eight ball in the corner pocket. The table was now clear except for the cue ball.

"Go for it, dude," she said.

Merton reached into his pocket and pulled out four quarters and examined them.

"How much is it to play here?"

"A buck-fifty," she said.

"Shit. Connie, do you got two quarters?"

Conrad reached into his pocket and pulled out his change. He picked out two quarters and handed them to Merton.

"Thanks, pal."

Merton pushed the little coin tray into the slot, and Conrad heard all the pool balls drop down to the far end of the table. Merton walked over and began pulling them out. He was careful in how he arranged them in the rack like there was a precise science to it. It was unclear whether he knew what he was doing or was just faking it. The blonde chick didn't seem impressed by his theatrics and started chalking up her stick.

While Conrad was staring at the scene, one of the women, a sweet and innocent-looking redhead, came over and sat down next to him.

"You're the quiet one, aren't you?" she said.

"Excuse me?"

The noise of the jukebox and their distance from the others made their conversation inaudible to everybody but themselves.

"I'm the same way," she said, not waiting for an answer.

"Oh, cool."

"I bet you like sci-fi."

"Oh, heck yeah. How can you tell?"

"I just can."

The tall blonde walked around to the open end of the table opposite Merton with her stick in one hand and the cue ball in the other. She placed it on the green felt and stared at the racked balls with a mathematician's precision. Suddenly she looked up at Merton.

"So, are we playing for anything?" She smiled seductively.

The question had such a sexual provocation; it seemed to throw Merton off.

"Sure, cocktails, eh?"

"I don't think I'm that thirsty. How about twenty dollars."

"Yeah, fine. That sounds cool."

The blonde walked over to the side table and rustled through her purse, pulling out a twenty-dollar bill, which she laid on the edge of the table. Merton reached into his back pocket and pulled out his wallet and did the same. He looked over at Conrad and winked. The wink was intended to be reassuring, but Conrad could see a world of fear behind it.

"My name is Claire," said the redhead, who was leaning into Conrad from the other side of their little square table.

"I'm Conrad."

"Hi. That's a sweet name. Your parents must be very cool."

"Yeah, they're good."

The blonde broke up the balls with a loud crack, and the three-ball fell into the far corner pocket. She walked over to the far side of the table where Merton was trying to stand casually but had a slightly rigid, ill ease about him. She knocked two more solids in and finally missed on a third shot, smiling at Merton with a hand gesture as if to say, "All yours."

It turned out Claire went to an all-girls college in New

Hampshire and majored in computer science with a minor in mathematics.

"You don't meet many female mathematicians," Conrad said. "That's very cool."

"You think so? Actually it was a minor, like I say, but I really enjoyed it. I can sometimes understand complicated physics lectures without needing a dumbed-down version for the layman."

"I would love that," Conrad said. He explained that he had studied accounting at a trade school but spent two years at a junior college beforehand. He was satisfied that he had an overall decent education but really respected people who dared to challenge themselves like Claire.

Merton was able to get a striped ball into the side pocket but scratched on the next shot, turning the table back over to the blonde, whose name was Jody.

"Excuse me, OK?" Claire said.

"Why, what?" asked Conrad.

"I have to use the lady's room."

"Oh, yeah. Go ahead."

Claire got up and walked behind the table to a little darkened vestibule behind the pool area, where there was a sign that read Restrooms. As soon as she disappeared, Merton sidled over to Conrad and leaned into his ear.

"What are you doing, man? She's the prop."

"The what?"

"The prop. The one that's not here to get laid."

"Oh. Well, I'll get to work on the other one as soon as your game's over."

"Well, don't waste any time, man. She'll be all over the first guy that shows interest in her."

Conrad looked at the woman. She had jet-black hair hung low and a slightly acned (though not unattractive) face but didn't look especially eager to find a mate. He wondered if maybe he was not good at reading the signs. He always suspected that anyway.

Jody knocked a solid into a side pocket and then missed on the next. She didn't look like she was really trying—she sort of "phoned-in" the shot, as they say. Conrad's attention was distracted as Claire stepped out of the bathroom. She seemed to have brushed her hair a bit and looked especially attractive to him. She came and sat down delicately, looked at him, and smiled.

"So," Conrad said, "Have you seen *The Pluto Crusaders*? It's on pay-per-view."

Claire gasped. "Yes! I saw it the other night. What a great story! So much bravery in the midst of such brutal contradictions."

"How so?"

"Have you seen it yet?"

"No."

"Well, I don't want to spoil the movie for you, but there's a scene early on when the crusaders' ship gets nicked by a meteor and it looks like all might be lost. Before they continue their journey, the Americans try to force the Israelis to accept Jesus Christ as their lord and savior so God won't kill them all. The Israelis refuse and, as you can imagine, it reveals a hypocrisy in everybody's agenda."

"I heard the Iranian colonists weren't nearly as bad as they were originally portrayed. They were just businessmen trying to get ahead."

"Well I can't tell you any more; you'll have to see it."

Jody had now cleared everything off the table but the eight ball, and Merton still had a couple of shots left. Again she seemed to be playing just lame enough to keep him interested. When Merton missed his next shot, she knocked the eight ball in and grabbed the forty dollars off the table.

"Another one?" Merton asked. "Double or nothing?"

"Let's make it for fifty," Jody said.

"Oooh, I like confident women."

Jody winked at him as Merton walked to the end of the table to rack up the balls. Once again, Jody broke and, once again, knocked the three-ball into the corner pocket.

"Hey," Claire asked. "Have you ever been to the Henrietta Swan Leavitt Planetarium?"

"No, but I hear it's amazing."

"Oh, God, the exhibits they have there are unbelievable. It's like being on board the Kepler telescope."

"Wow, that's so cool."

Jody knocked a couple of balls in and then missed (again almost playfully) and turned the table over to Merton.

Conrad could see that Merton had taken on a deep seriousness and was even perspiring a little. He looked back at Claire and saw that her glass was empty.

"What are you drinking?"

"White wine."

"Oh cool. Can I get you another?"

"Sure that would be great."

"Merton," he said. "Do you want another gin and tonic?"

"Yeah, yeah, whatever." Merton was concentrating hard on a corner shot that struck Conrad as being somewhat routine.

He walked over to the bar and ordered drinks for the three of them. He hadn't asked Jody or the other gal and felt a little stupid, but when he looked back he noticed they both had full bottles of beer. Instead of having another Bud—his first one was still half full on the table—Conrad had a glass of white wine too. When he returned to the table with the drinks, Claire had a puzzled expression on her face.

"You bought me two glasses?"

"No, no, one's for me. It's what I wanted originally. I don't know why I ordered a Budweiser."

"Maybe to look like a man. That's what a lot of guys at this place are about."

Conrad laughed. "Yeah, I guess a little."

"You don't really fit into a place like this, Conrad."

"I sometimes wonder if I fit in anywhere."

"Yeah, I know what you're saying. I mean, I like goofing around, but I can't imagine making a place like this my one and only focus in life."

"No shit."

Conrad looked back over at the game and noticed that Jody had cleared off most of the solids while Merton still had all but one of his balls on the table. He and Claire both watched quietly as Jody again started phoning in her shots and missing to let Merton catch up. Finally, when Merton only had a pair of stripes left, she knocked in her last ball and made a terrific bank shot on the eight ball.

"One more," Merton said.

"Are you sure?"

"Hell yeah. A hundred bucks this time. I have to get some money from the ATM though."

"OK. Do what you gotta."

Merton walked out of the pool area to the front of the bar. Jody was staring at him pitifully and then looked over at the black-haired woman, who was inspecting her nails. She looked up at Jody, and they both laughed.

"Hey, do you want to take a walk?" Claire asked.

Conrad nodded his head, and the two of them got up and grabbed their jackets.

Claire called over to Jody, "Hey, don't let anyone grab our wine glasses. We'll be back."

"No problem."

The two of them walked out of the pool area and were just passing Merton at the ATM.

"Hey," he said. "Where you goin'? The party's just getting started."

"We'll be back," Conrad said.

When they stepped out of the door into the cool evening, Conrad and Claire stared at each other and started to laugh. They stood in the reflection of the marquee's yellow neon lasso, and, after a moment, both instinctually stepped into each other and kissed. It was a long, slow kiss, and when their lips and bodies pulled away, there was something else that didn't.

"We definitely have to do that planetarium thing together," Claire said.

"Hell, I could *live* there."

"Me too!"

They laughed again and kissed. This time it was even more passionate. It was like the pressure of a birthing star in a stellar nebula. When they pulled away, Claire grabbed Conrad's hand, and they started down the boulevard in a purposeful stroll. He let go of her hand and reached his arm around her; she did the same. With her free hand she pointed up to the night sky in front of them. The stars were mostly obscured, but some were visible.

"Check it out—Orion!" she said.

Conrad smiled. He forgot about the wine and the pool match as they walked into the starry horizon.